THE CHILDREN'S ROOM

THE
CHILDREN'S
ROOM

LOUIS-RENE DES FORÊTS

Translated from the French by
Jean Stewart

LONDON
JOHN CALDER

PUBLISHED IN GREAT BRITAIN BY
JOHN CALDER (PUBLISHERS) LTD.
17 SACKVILLE ST., LONDON, W.I.

PRINTED IN GREAT BRITAIN
BY CLARKE, DOBLE AND BRENDON LTD.
CATTEDOWN, PLYMOUTH

CONTENTS

THE BAVARD

THE BAVARD

I OFTEN look at myself in the glass. My greatest desire has always been to discover something poignant about the expression in my eyes. I think I have always preferred to those women who, either because they were blinded with love or as a means of holding me, pretended that I was really handsome or had striking features, those who whispered with a sort of timid hesitancy that I wasn't quite like other people. Indeed, I convinced myself for a long time that the most attractive thing about me must be my singularity. This sense of being different provided my chief sources of exaltation. But now that I have lost a little of my conceit, how can I disguise from myself the fact that I am utterly undistinguished? I cannot write this without a grimace. It's bad enough that I should at last have learnt this intolerable truth, but that you should know it too! . . . To be honest, my embarrassment is tinged with that slight feeling of bitter pleasure that one always gets from exhibiting any of one's defects, even if it should not have the slightest chance of interesting other people. I may perhaps be asked whether I have undertaken to confess myself in order to enjoy this somewhat morbid pleasure, which I might compare to that derived by certain very sensitive people from slowly stroking with their finger-tip a slight scratch they have deliberately made on their lower lip, or from pressing the end of their tongue against the pulp of an unripe lemon. At this I cannot help smiling, and it is with a smile that I reply that I pride myself on having small liking for confessions; my friends say that I am silence itself, and they will not deny that, for all their cunning, they have never been able to extract from me what I had resolved to keep secret. This inability of mine to confide in anyone has even been considered a serious failing, deserving of pity, and I cannot resist the pleasure, identical with that I have described above, of adding that some secret vanity impelled me to take advantage of this belief by feigning, or merely exaggerating, the distress caused by this deplorable affliction, as though I had some great secret which I should have found relief in confiding, if I had not considered it, by reason of its exceptional and at the same time intimate character, quite impossible to confess.

But if I let my zeal run away with me I shall end by ascribing to myself ulterior motives which I have never had, in order to pass for a sincere man who does not seek to spare himself humiliations. It is therefore not for the pleasure of talking about myself that I have taken up my pen, nor yet to show off my literary gifts. Here I am obliged to open a parenthesis, but you must have found out by experience that as soon as one tries to explain oneself frankly, one is forced to follow up every affirmation by a phrase expressing doubt, which is usually equivalent to denying what one has just stated, in short, it's impossible to shed one's exasperating scruples about leaving anything in the dark. I was saying then that I am not in the least concerned about the form in which I put these lines on paper. 'Not in the least' is perhaps going too far. My natural tendency is towards a highly-coloured style, allusive, passionate, scornful and sombre, and today I have resolved, with a certain reluctance, to lay aside any studied refinement of form, so that I am now

writing in a style which is not my own; that's to say I have
discarded all the trumpery attractions at my disposal, although
I am not a little proud of them. (Take care, after 'although'
there's a tiny lie; I know that my attractions are merely the
fruit of a quite commonplace cleverness.) Add to this that my
natural style is not that of the confessional, and there's nothing
to wonder at if it's like a host of others, but I've no pretensions
on that score, and you have been warned.

Let's get down to the reasons, then, that have led to this sordid
self-analysis. You'll notice, by the way, the somewhat banter-
ing tone I've lapsed into, in spite of my resolve to be both
serious and sincere, neither aggressive nor seductive, but if you
try the same experiment you will discover that there is nothing
harder, unless one is excited by some conviction, than to talk
about oneself in all gravity, leaving aside all the pleasures of
insolence; you'll find yourself afraid of ridicule and, however
conscientiously you may bare your soul, a vein of irrepressible
irony will aways make itself felt. A coward conceals the truth
under the ambiguous shield of insolence or banter : you despise
me, reader, but you can surely see that I'm exaggerating my
vices : it's up to you to work out a compromise; nothing prevents you from taking all this as the invention of an exhibition-
ist whose actions, if not his thoughts, are ingenuous and blame-
less. Now let's get down to those reasons. Actually there's only
one, and I must say it is in the highest degree comic.

I suppose most of you have had the experience of being
buttonholed by one of those garrulous fellows who, longing
to make their voices heard, seek out a companion whose only
function is to lend an ear, without any obligation to utter a

word; and indeed it's not even certain that the bore insists on being listened to, it's enough to assume an air of being interested, either by giving an occasional nod or what novelists call a murmur of approval, or by valiantly enduring the poor beggar's insistent gaze despite the exhaustion inevitably ensuing from such a muscular strain. Let's take a closer look at such a man. That he should feel the need to speak and yet have nothing to say, and moreover that he cannot satisfy this need without the more or less tacit complicity of a companion chosen by him, if he's been free to choose, for qualities of discretion and endurance, these facts are worth pondering over. This fellow has nothing whatsoever to say, and yet he says a thousand things; he doesn't really mind whether his interlocutor agrees with or dissents from him, and yet he cannot do without him, although he wisely requires from him only a purely formal attention. It all takes place as if he were affected by a disease for which he can find no remedy or, to borrow a familiar comparison, as if he were in the same dilemma as the Sorcerer's Apprentice : the machine goes round to no purpose, and he is unable to control its wayward movements. Now I make bold to say, at the risk of instantly alienating all my readers, that I belong to this particular brand of talkers.

But, for the benefit of those who have gone on reading in spite of so deplorable a revelation, I feel bound to look further back to the origins of my affliction, although I find it almost impossibly difficult to describe it and to convey its nature to my readers if they have never known it.

To begin with, the highly suggestive character of the atmosphere and the place in which I experienced my first attack, which I shall try to relate, would doubtless justify a meticulous description, such as only a writer concerned with arousing the emotions of his readers and expert in this field, endowed moreover by nature with gifts to which I make no pretension, would be capable of providing. For myself, it would involve breaking the vow I have made to myself not to resort to dishonest literary expedients which repel me.

It was late one Sunday afternoon, when I was feeling particularly bored and depressed, that I suddenly decided to leave my room and go for a swim on the neighbouring beach. I felt a longing to dive, to swallow a mouthful of sea, to shake the salt water from my head and then to swim rhythmically, to turn over and float, to feel the cold swell lift me and sink with me and the sun burn my face. But first I had to go up and then down, to cross a river and a dense wooded valley, then reach the long plateau and cross that, through the long grass that made walking difficult, then go up again and down again and across again, stopping sometimes in the shade of a tree to get my breath, and then go up and down and across again, forcing my way through dense brambles in the woodland, all this under a scorching sun, before reaching the chalk cliff above the beach. I got so hot going up and down those hills and crossing those thick woods that I lay down on the crest of the cliff, and I was happy to lean my back against the trunk of a lonely pine that covered me with its fresh, fragrant shadow. I stayed there a long time, day-dreaming in my own way, quite inconsequentially, probably the way dogs do when you leave them alone and they don't want to go hunting or to wag their tails or even to doze, and for me, as presumably for dogs, such moments are all the more delectable in that they occur so rarely. I wanted nothing now except to lie without moving and wait for night to fall. Looking up at the sky, which was utterly blue with a very few white clouds driven by the wind, and feeling at a distance the heat of the sun on the white rock, I was happy as you are when you've left all your domestic worries behind you and are at last in possession of something you like, which makes you feel good, and quite alone, and remote from all that seems so important in men's eyes. Yes, that was what I felt most strongly, that I was remote from man and that men's worries were absolutely devoid of significance. I would not dwell thus on the state of euphoria I was enjoying, had I not had cause to believe, an hour later, that it was the prologue and, somehow, the source of the first manifestation of my complaint in its active form. Lying under the pine tree, I stared at the sky for a long while, absorbed in purely animal contemplation, steeped in utter peace and convinced that anything that might happen to me that evening was bound to be for the best. But when I noticed that the sky was no longer as clear nor the air as warm, and that the murmur of the sea was already more distant, since the tide was lowest at the close of day, my serenity gave place to a strange excitement which took the form of a frantic need to make a speech immediately, although I felt no concern as to whether this speech would make sense and even less as to what its theme should be; I was a prey to such violent agitation that I sprang to my feet precipitately. However, I never uttered that speech; my lips remained obstinately closed and I stood there in silence waiting for this oratorical thirst to abate of itself. But the longer I waited the greater grew my discomfort. To make myself understood I can only compare it to that of a man who, feeling ill at ease after too copious a meal, tries in vain to resort to the swiftest method of relieving himself.

Actually this attack lasted only a short time, and no sooner had it vanished than I thought no more about it; I promptly recovered my calm of mind but not, unfortunately, the delicious exaltation which had preceded it. Moreover, when I underwent a fresh attack a few days later, I had to resign myself most unwillingly to enduring it without previously enjoying that rapture, which I have attempted to describe as best I could, and which I at first considered indissolubly linked, like cause and effect, to that distress that had followed it, and I reflected bitterly that if they had only been associated by chance, one would have amply compensated for the other. To go back to the actual nature of this attack, it is remarkable that it should have taken the form of a strange longing to hold forth, which I found impossible to satisfy, but the fact is that words would not come to my aid; in short, I wanted to talk and had absolutely nothing to say.

It is so much my habit to consider my failings as rare diseases on which no treatment has any effect, and whose course I must watch with helpless curiosity, that a sort of disillusioned indifference seems to me, to some extent, the most reasonable attitude to take in face of the phenomenon I have described. In fact there is something absurd about the way I persist in considering myself a sick man when I am depressed, or consumed by gloomy jealousy, or when some new revelation of my inadequacy makes me want to bury myself underground, or when ambition frets me, or vanity—all those failings, in short, to which I am frequently subject and against which I unfortunately have no remedy, being afflicted with a total lack of will power and never, at any time, enjoying that unselfconsciousness common to many happy men, which seems to me by

far the most enviable of qualities. When I am in the slough of
despond, I don't struggle to get out of it, I stay in it up to my
neck. It is true, as I said at the beginning, that I have often
been teased about my taciturn nature, and then pitied for it;
here again, I was inclined to discern in this inability to unburden myself all the symptoms of an incurable disease and,
what is far more significant, it was impossible for my friends
themselves, witnessing the anguish that my face betrayed while
they strove in vain to extract my confidences, not to be struck
by the analogy between the state in which they saw me and
that of a sick man driven in on himself by internal suffering.
But in the present case, if my anguish was essentially connected with my incapacity to satisfy a burning desire, it differed
from that earlier anguish by the very nature of its causes. In my
friends' company, the problem was that of self-expression; on
the cliffs, merely that of chattering at random, regardless of
logic or coherence. It was one thing to be unable to communicate and thereby to be deprived of the pleasure of pure and
sincere friendship, but quite another to suffer from an apparently organic deficiency whose most obvious result was to
repress a vice that might be dangerous and was, in any case,
sterile, since I did not feel I could derive from it that vital satisfaction that we seek through confiding in another person. But
still the two experiences had at least one thing in common :
anguish. And yet, after several consecutive experiences which
were not noticeably different from that which I have described
and on which it is superfluous to enlarge here, I presently
underwent a far more violent and indeed spectacular attack,
significantly akin to those which so disastrously affected the
relations I wished to maintain with my friends.

To protect myself against the smiles of those who, on the strength of my own admission that I am apt to affect singularity, might be inclined to doubt the veracity of this story, I cannot do better than resort to utter sobriety, somewhat reluctantly rejecting the hallucinatory power of certain images that haunt my mind and any pursuit of effects which, though desirable, have through their association with fiction become suspect in the eyes of those readers who are sticklers for objectivity. It may be the better for me in the long run : I intend to avoid any attempt to transpose, gloss over or touch up the facts and stick to an absolutely faithful reproduction of them; I should not object, even if my pedantry should lay me open to ridicule, to being considered a serious-minded person or even, if I should go too far, a somewhat comically serious one. Now I invite anyone who wants to laugh to do so openly; I want them to know that I am only too ready to join in their laughter. All I need is to believe that somebody does me the honour of paying attention to me. Who? I don't care! Anyone, if only a reader whose boredom makes him inattentive.

I must admit that until then, neither my friends nor my relatives had troubled to find out what had given me those drawn features, that pallor, those nervous and uncertain gestures. Perhaps they were completely devoid of perspicacity, perhaps they did not worry about my heath, and that suited me perfectly. God knows what agony it is, when you are suffering from an affliction you want to keep secret, to hear people comment on your appearance and ask you if you're feeling all right or if something's the matter with you, and you get out of it by joking about the foul cold you've caught or something equally inoffensive, and you mustn't show that you're thinking :

does that satisfy you, do you know all you want to? But when your real friends start really worrying, even if you're a very expert liar, it's hard to conceal what is in fact the matter with you, because they'll never believe you unless the explanation you offer is in keeping with your appearance or your attitude and actually quite as serious as the one you're trying to conceal, but then it would have cost you far less to tell the truth right away. In fact, have you got any friends who mind about what happens to you? If you haven't, I think after all you're maybe lucky. But this is really a pointless digression, since nobody had even told me I looked unwell until the day when, yielding to the attraction which, these last few years, a bottle or a single glass of alcohol has had for me, I was rash enough to get drunk in public.

The critical phase of my attack took place in a sort of dance hall into which I had drifted with a few friends who, having already drunk a fair amount, had decided to go and have a good time somewhere, despite the strong objections I had raised, having always detested anything remotely resembling debauchery; but I realised that they were so much further gone than myself that they were incapable of seeing the foolishness of this, and from the serious way in which they talked of paying a visit to a place of even worse reputation, which I dare not name here, I saw that I should have to drink a fair amount in order to reach their level of intoxication and join wholeheartedly in their unwholesome pleasures. They teased me because I only took part in the conversation to give grand-motherly advice, they'd rather have my everlasting silence than such moral lectures, and in any case I was far too sober to say anything sensible. I swallowed their sarcasms with a smile, but

I was vexed. One glance around me was enough to show that
it was useless and possibly dangerous to persist, and I therefore decided to retreat into that silence which they had so
ungraciously recommended.

The tavern which we entered, our faces reddened by a wind
as keen as a knife-edge, our hair covered with snow and our
shoes wet, was occupied by the densest swarm of men and
women dancing, or laughing over their drinks, that I had ever
seen. I must confess that I was delighted with the noisy laughter, the sound of shuffling feet, the various shouted remarks,
often of the coarsest nature, above which you could scarcely
hear the band's shrill music spattering the walls, and with the
throng of revellers dancing and drinking in so narrow a space
that it seemed impossible to squeeze in a fresh customer; if I
did not immediately feel at my ease in this turbid atmosphere
(the fact is that one so much expects to see in a place like this
one definite category of individuals, that the intrusive appearance of individuals belonging to a different category, like my
friends and myself, seems unusual and even startling until the
moment when, by some extraordinary mimesis, you realise that
you are breathing this alien atmosphere as naturally as if no
other could be more familiar to you; on reflection, it would be
truer to say that, on crossing the threshold, you are aware, for
a limited length of time, of a current of hostility towards yourself, the intruder), at all events I had reason to think that I
should pass unnoticed there, and I realised with delight that I
should be unable to talk to other people, since they could not
possibly hear me. This was a good thing. I would sit apart,
indifferent to the jokes that would be made about my never
opening my mouth; it was pleasant to think that I could in all

quietude enjoy the pleasure of watching a bit of life without
being required to take part in it; all that I wanted now was to
stay in one corner, surrounded by smoke and music and
laughter and yet solitary, watching avidly and clearsightedly
an animated scene in which I alone, to my great satisfaction,
took no active part. As a child I used to experience a singular
and somewhat enigmatic delight in wandering idly among the
swings and switchbacks at a fair, my hands in my pockets, to
watch, with an eagerness as inexhaustible as if I were myself
actively involved, the rowdy enjoyment of children of my own
age, shrieking with delighted anguish on the swings—and I
shuddered for fear these might accidentally whirl right round
over the bar to which they were fixed—or else astride their
wooden horses, one hand clutching the rod outstretched towards a ring which had to be unhooked in time—and my own
fingers trembled in my pocket, as if they had themselves grown
clumsy through exhaustion or fear of failure. To active pleasure, which I often felt to be a constraint or an illusion, too
limited or else inaccessible, I preferred what seemed to me the
incomparably more powerful delight I derived from the sight
of collective joy expressed in various ways by the faces on which
I gazed, fascinated. It was strictly a matter of sympathy, a
sympathy which enabled me to get inside the pleasure of others
and experience it with an intensity which was all the keener and
more persistent because I shared that pleasure with a great
number of children at once and in succession, all the deeper
because by somehow escaping the bewilderment due to the
violent attractions of the outside world, I was able to savour
my pleasure in privacy and lucidity and to dominate it instead
of submitting to it. Even today I find it hard to resist seizing the

first opportunity of hurrying to the scene of any popular demonstration, where I might be in a position to observe on people's faces all the characteristic signs of passion—caring little whether it be aroused by foolish admiration or unjustified resentment; only the fear of being myself carried away by a powerful stream of anger or enthusiasm, by reason of my very faculty of sympathy and despite the self-control I have vowed to maintain, sometimes prevents me from yielding to this impulse. My curiosity is so great that I willingly shut myself up in a stuffy cinema in the hope—generally disappointed—of watching a close-up of a really expressive face.

If from all this it clearly emerges that I belong in the category of those pitiful fellows known as *voyeurs,* the reader is entitled to be shocked, but how can he be sure that I am not letting my imagination run away with me? Prove to me that I am telling the truth. Are you suggesting that such a lie would do me no good? And suppose I'm telling lies for the pleasure of lying, and suppose I choose to write this rather than that, namely a lie rather than the truth, or to be precise whatever comes into my head, and suppose I ask nothing better than to be judged on a false confession, suppose, in fact, that I thoroughly enjoy ruining my own reputation? But I can see your answer coming : it's too easy to attenuate the disagreeable effect of a confession by implying that it may be called in question. Very well, I'll let you have the last word. But I was careful, at the beginning, to preclude any misunderstanding by stating clearly that my sole concern was to convince myself that I had a reader. Just one. And a reader, I insist, means somebody who reads, not necessarily somebody who judges. Not that I absolutely object to being judged, but if the reader is

dying of impatience and boredom I entreat him not to show
it. I'd like him to know, once and for all, that I don't want
yawns and sighs, muttered exclamations and petulant stamp-
ing; can I help it if I've a preference for well-mannered
people? And note that I'm not asking you to read me *really*,
but to maintain me in the illusion that I'm being read; do you
get the subtle difference?—So you talk for the sake of lying?
—No, sir, for the sake of talking, nothing more; and isn't that
what you yourself do from morning till night, and not merely
to your cat? And does a writer write for any other reason than
because he wants to write? But enough of that. I object to
being muttered at while I'm talking.

Although it seemed to me necessary, in order to maintain
the pleasant state I was in, to preserve all my mental alertness
intact, I had enough experience of my own weakness to fore-
tell with absolute certainty that no consideration of this sort
would restrain me from yielding to the absurd and immediate
temptation of emptying that glass I saw glittering in front of me;
and I even believe that it was the certainty of imminent downfall that impelled me to forestall that event. I drank four glasses
in quick succession, and that was very pleasant too. The best
justification for my weakness seemed to me to lie in the fact
that my sensitivity, instead of growing confused, became both
clearer and more receptive, and I felt full of sympathy,
tremendous sympathy, for all these restless people. How right
they were to laugh and dance and drink, and prepare by word
and gesture for making love! What a useful way to spend their
time! The whole secret of life consists in the sight of these hope-
ful or despairing people, in love or seeking love, in this shatter-
ing din, in this warm stuffy atmosphere, I told myself, raising

my glass. To live means to feel, and to drink, dance and laugh means to feel, so living consists of drinking, dancing and laughter; and with this delightful syllogism I emptied my glass. It was marvellous to see tipsy people dancing and it was marvellous to be a little tipsy oneself. But the fact is that I was completely drunk. Sitting at a little zinc table in a noisy corner, I listened to the talk going on all round me, and through the blue haze of cigarette smoke I watched the couples go past me one after the other, trying to catch scraps of conversation on the way, but this was unnecessary : a person's looks and bearing told me more than his words; if a woman were the object of my scrutiny, I allowed myself one approving glance at her figure before passing on to her face, which I studied fervently and which in most cases revealed the passions unleashed by the excitement of the dance, the prevailing atmosphere or the hope of some conquest, an excitement by which I was myself affected to the point of ecstasy and dizziness, for just as the dazzling reflection of the sun on a pure white surface is far more painful to the eye than the direct perception of the sun itself, so the spectacle of another's pleasure owes its contagious power and its emotive value, I believe, to the fact that this pleasure, giving radiance to the very flesh of another's face, takes on the completely convincing character of sensuous experience. But when my gaze, at this point, met that of a very beautiful woman dancing in the arms of an absurdly short fellow with a hooked nose and red hair rising in two unequal waves on either side of a faultless parting, cut across the middle by the peak of a cap stuck on the back of his head, I immediately had the comforting feeling that there was someone else in the room who, behind an inexpressive mask, fed secretly on the pleasure of others

with an avidity as feverish and deliberate as my own. If I suddenly felt unable to detach my gaze from that of the woman
who, moreover, seemed quite undisturbed by the interest which,
under the stimulus of intoxication, I displayed with over-bold
persistence, it was because her eyes, her face and her whole
manner were in curious contrast with those of the other women,
who were laughing provocatively and casting alluring glances
over their partner's shoulder at the handful of men sitting
around, carelessly showing their naked thighs and ceaselessly
calling out to one another remarks whose broadness was only
justified by the peculiar nature of the place and the vulgar
tastes of its clientele. I feel no shame in admitting that after
so many drinks I had become less and less capable of distinguishing this woman from her neighbours, and that in any case
there may have been nothing about her which entitled me to
suppose, naïvely, that she was enjoying the same sort of pleasure as myself : nothing, possibly, on her handsome face that
suggested a more refined enjoyment than that of the rest. But
I chose to interpret her reserved manner, so strikingly unlike
the surrounding exuberance, in a way which may quite well
have been mistaken. However, this probably illusory impression that my pleasure was in all respects similar to that in
which I imagined her to be secretly indulging arose not only
from that unusual reserve : there was her partner too, that
little redhaired fellow clinging to her and raising ardent eyes
towards her almost lifeless face, heaving sighs and expressing
sentiments to which she seemed to pay no attention. Perhaps
because he talked incessantly and she never uttered a word,
and because he stared at her persistently while she let her
eyes roam far and wide above his head, deliberately exclud-

ing him from her interest in a way which would have discouraged anybody less infatuated, she seemed to me to be far
more occupied with the pleasure of others than with that which
her partner was pressing on her with such fruitless patience
and fervour.

But all this is an unnecessarily roundabout way of saying
a simple thing: I wanted to dance with her. And I am forced
to admit that this desire was really based on the gravity of her
expression and, still more, on the purely physical attraction
of her admirably proportioned body, and not at all, as I've
been pointlessly striving to make out, on my astonishment at
the similarity—probably created out of nothing by my in-
ebriated imagination—between her recipe for pleasure and my
own. Moreover, it was surely by a dishonest afterthought that
I substituted for the desire I felt to hold this woman in my
arms, the rapture I should have enjoyed at discovering someone else in that room who differed from the rest by the way in
which, like myself, she knew how to extract the greatest possible variety of effects from pleasure. But after all, what does it
matter to you? Did I desire her physically, or did she merely
excite my curiosity by her serious expression? Does anyone
want to know the precise reasons that made me get up and
ask her for the next dance? I cannot think whence men derive
that surprising love of truth, for which they usually have no
use, why they go into such raptures on reading a report whose
clarity and concision, so they say, are the best guarantees of
the authenticity of the facts it relates. We are not here, thank
God, to pursue an endlessly elusive truth, which could be an
exercise as maddening to the mind as, for instance, the effort
of threading a needle with thick black cotton would be to the

hand. And yet I must admit, and in any case I've no wish to disguise the fact, that neither the passionate interest I felt in her enigmatic air (from which I carefully avoided drawing any hasty conclusions) nor the peculiar and purely accidental position in which I then found myself, would suffice to explain my sudden desire to hold this woman in my arms for at least the space of one dance, but, need I repeat it, I merely felt that it would be good to hold that body close to my own and to see those grey eyes fixed on mine and to hear in my ears the murmur of that voice whose tones must be so striking. In any case, it's of no importance as regards subsequent events, and you may be sure that if I go in for all this analysis and hypo-thesis it's less from a scrupulous concern to lose nothing of the thoughts that came flooding into my mind, than because I enjoy playing a harmless little game at which I don't pretend to be a past master : that game which consists of first keeping your interlocutor in suspense and then bewildering him with what might have happened, what may have happened, what surely never happened, what ought to have happened and what couldn't help happening and what you've forgotten to say and what you've said that was not so, and so on until, his patience at an end, he cries out : 'Keep to the point!' and by this furious call to order lets you know that you haven't com-pletely wasted your time.

As soon as the music stopped I rose and, to the great surprise of my friends, who up till now had entirely ignored me, I went straight to the young woman and asked her to dance with me. Before she had time to accept, the redheaded fellow broke in, declaring in an insolent and peremptory tone that the next dance was also his. But I disregarded his claims and, quickly seizing the girl by the waist, I drew her into the middle of the room, where we began to dance. He followed us, pushing his way between the dancers; he had no intention of letting go, and he called on me in highly discourteous tones to give back what didn't belong to me. I asked him politely if she were his personal property. No? In that case I advised him to mind his own business and I added that I must warn him I was a bit drunk, not completely drunk but just enough to lose my self-control. Wild with rage, he protested more loudly, his eager frantic stare fixed on the girl who was gazing with blank indifference across the room, his hoarse voice trembling with fury at the enormity of the wrong I had done him. I told him to shut up, and begged him to stop this silly farce; he should take the matter more calmly; turn and turn about, would he mind dancing with that melancholy fat girl in the corner over there, waiting for some kind person to ask her? These last words intensified his fury. Pale-faced, his fists clenched, the very picture of a flouted lover, he was obviously preparing to separate us by force, and I made ready to parry the first blows and return with interest any he might succeed in giving me. At this point the young woman, abandoning her distant look, gave him a cold and haughty glare with her dark eyes, and let fly in Spanish a volley of presumably very biting remarks, which left him dumbfounded, and from the crestfallen and submissive way in which he dropped his eyes I realised that he was ready to give up the struggle. He stood there for a moment, wondering what to do with his hands, his face now expressing a merely formal anger. He just looked at each of us in turn with his mouth open; then he took a few steps backward to avoid being hemmed in by two dancing couples, and came up to us when we were on the edge of the dance floor to stammer out that after all she was free to make an exhibition of herself with any whippersnapper that came along. 'That's fine, thank you,' I said in a sarcastic tone, 'thanks very much!' He shrugged his shoulders, turned his back on us and went off to subside at a table with the deflated, hangdog look of a man who's been sent packing. A little while later I noticed that he was still slumped on his chair in front of a three-quarters-empty bottle, his red head aglow under the glare of an electric lamp and his fingers clasped round it like a crown, his eyes half closed between glistening lids, his face attentive and yet distorted by latent anger. I cannot swear that he was keeping watch on us, and yet he certainly had his eye on us. He had practically never ceased peering at us, consumed no doubt by intolerable shame, his outward calm concealing feelings that every instant grew more manifestly hostile towards the rival who deprived him of his only pleasure and humiliated him in front of the woman he loved.

I detest this sort of quarrel, naturally, yet I can find certain excuses for it under the circumstances : the strange fascination this woman exercised over me, the wholly unaccustomed strength of my desire, together with the state of semi-intoxication I was in after drinking eight glasses of strong liquor, all this enhanced by the unheard-of excitement which, during the whole time that I held her in my arms, succeeded in delivering me from the anguish to which I am condemned almost continuously by the feeling of irremediable loneliness.

Once the girl was close to me and her lover out of the way, I was free to immerse myself in the pleasure that swept caressingly over me : a pleasure so impetuous and overwhelming

that it made me forget my longing to hear her voice. Gazing
into one another's eyes, we danced without uttering a word. If
her nostrils quivered, if her eyes glittered with very dark fire,
if my hand felt a slow shudder run through her body as
though under some exquisite torture, nevertheless I saw on
her lips an ambiguous smile which seemed not to betoken
treachery so much as a disturbing complicity made even more
evident by the silence we maintained amidst the din that surrounded us. Perhaps the suspicious oddity of my behaviour,
my lurching gait, my dishevelled appearance may have put
her on her guard, perhaps she was trying to warn me by a
slight, ironical sign that she was not completely taken in by
the declarations I might feel impelled to make her and for
which my drunken state would account in large measure;
nonetheless, possessed by a wonderful ecstasy which prevented
me from imagining any possible disparity between our mutual
feelings and which endowed me with an illusory sense of in-
vulnerability, I felt no concern as to what she thought about
me, and this indifference is worth noting in view of the fact
that no pursuit excites me more than tracking down, by dint
of observation, perspicacity and cunning, the impression I
have made on people I love or at least whose good esteem I
value.

I am not one of those who are indifferent to a pretty
woman's opinion. The task of mentally organising, regroup-
ing or dovetailing the various comments made about me by a
particular person, whether spoken in my presence or retailed
second-hand, and then to reconstruct them into a fairly lifelike
picture which, whether flattering or unfavourable, never quite
corresponds to the permanent reality of what I am, is renewed

at each fresh contact I make, and constitutes for me the most
agonising of ordeals. The natural lucidity that I bring to it
never allows me to cheat by eluding what might be too painful to me; even when I find it difficult to reduce some favourable item to its correct proportions, I am not taken in, having
a profound contempt for any sort of self-deception. But my
embarrassment and awkwardness are all the keener, while the
disappointment most frequently aroused by so deformed an
image of myself (on which, it must be confessed, my natural
pessimism has left its unobtrusive mark) fosters the ambiguity
and, at the same time, confirms my conviction that the only
part of myself which I consider of real importance is forever
hidden from the eyes of those I love best, whereas whatever
else I may display is unimportant, and so I shall never be
understood, *understood* being equivalent to *loved* in my mind;
and this is a cruel realisation, with something obviously absurd
about it over which I occasionally laugh. But that day I was
decidedly very different from myself. Entirely absorbed by
that intoxicating pleasure in which, most unexpectedly, I had
begun to lose my footing, it never occurred to me to interpret
that smile, to examine it on all sides, nor to try and extract
from it those elements exclusively which might serve for the
subsequent construction of a more or less veracious image, and
it was far better so. In other circumstances the excessive importance I should have attached to the impression I was making and the embarrassment this would have caused me would
have allowed me no chance of freeing myself, for a brief
moment, from my inward torment, and my delight would
have been much diminished thereby, if not completely
poisoned. Now it was enough for me to feel this woman close

to me for everything to become clear and simple : no anxiety, no diffidence, no gloomy foreboding of probable failure; I was submerged in a perfect bliss which must be that experienced by madmen of a certain type at the climax of their attacks; in any case I think it is practically inexpressible. I looked at that face and never had I seen one so splendid, so ardent and yet so cold (I imagine that some of these purely external contradictions, which were so striking in this woman, played a large part in the power she had over me), so close to me that I identified my joy with the joy that it seemed to express— and yet remote enough to impose respect upon me and to arouse a curiosity with which there mingled a desire all the more ardent because its object seemed so inaccessible.

When the music stopped once more, I asked her to have a drink with me; she accepted with a smile, but no sooner had we sat down than her friend came up and invited her to dance; she shook her head without looking at him; he broke out into imprecations, then pleaded his cause in Spanish with despairing fervour; she paid not the slightest attention but sat in silence, with the same sharp smile on her lips. Realising that it was futile to try and persuade her, and enraged at feeling himself cheated, he turned towards me and marched on me with his fists raised and a look of vicious animosity; instinctively I drew back, sliding my chair over the floor, and took up a defensive attitude somewhat prematurely, with a clumsiness that was no doubt highly comic. But fearing presumably that he might do me some injury, the young woman intervened, urging him in a calm, slow and resolute voice to go back to his table, where she would join him presently; at least that was what I understood her to say. This injunction at first only provoked him to strange silent gesticulation, accompanied by strangled sounds. His mouth was half open, his thick lips seemed swollen; his bloodshot eyes, gleaming with resentment and rage, tried to probe the depths of the young woman's calm dark gaze, while she scrutinised the bitter bewildered face of her victim, with an expression of curiosity as to the effects of her power but without being able to repress a kind of impatience, betrayed by the nervous drumming of her fingers on the edge of the table. Meanwhile I sat watching this horrible scene in silence, with a singular unawareness of its humiliating implications for myself, accepting, with a lightheartedness that seems staggering to me today, the eviction of my adversary by such a piece of feminine treachery, not to mention the hatred which he would unfailingly bear towards me, the consequences of which I should shortly have to endure. The fact is that I could not help feeling an intense delight in the twofold spectacle presented by, on the one hand, the anguished, puzzled face of the defeated man who, secretly maddened by the helplessness to which his devouring passion reduced him, could not quite conceal a sort of cold rage (and I felt quite unmoved by the fact that it was directed against myself), and on the other hand the mysterious smile, the disarming gaze, the commanding air and proud bearing of the woman, who knew how to keep her pining lover at a distance when she wanted others to pay court to her. I mistook myself for a spectator when it was quite evident that I was one of the actors, the least interesting of the three by reason of the cowardly and passive attitude in which I persisted. However, keen as is my wish for sincerity, I am not going to sacrifice my good name unfairly in its interests; I think I may say that I did not indulge in this inertia out of insensitivity, effrontery or scepticism, nor even out of cowardice in the face of that threatening anger. Actually nothing could be more authentic than the feeling of calm relaxation and euphoria that overwhelmed me, enlivened only by a touch of curiosity which, after all, was quite legitimate. Moreover, although this excuse strikes me as a poor one today (but in whose eyes am I so anxious to justify myself? You have already noticed the *keen as is my wish for sincerity*) I think it fair to add that I was in a hypersensitive state due to excessive drinking, which partially explains the strangeness of my behaviour. I don't think I was fully aware of things. I was doing my best to appear completely at my ease, and presumably I could not have endured watching that fellow suffer in front of me and on account of me if I had not previously drained several glasses of brandy and soda. I considered what was happening in front of me most interesting. Why did the redheaded man stand there looking like a child about to burst into tears? In his place I'd have smashed in the face of that rotten pimp, myself, but I had forgotten that I myself was that rotten pimp. I felt far removed from what I was watching with such avid curiosity, and completely irresponsible, as irresponsible as is a worthy bourgeois at the theatre with regard to the gory tragedy being enacted a few yards in front of him. All that I wanted to do just then was to sit back in my chair and quietly enjoy the passionate, cruel and drink-crazed aspect of the situation. Naturally there was no question of my intervening.

But, lulled by my pleasant euphoria, I did not suspect that I was about to become the principal actor, in fact the only actor in the next scene, which I promised earlier to describe to

c

you with the strict and impassive exactitude of a medical
report, provided I don't let myself be carried away by the
emotion that I might feel on remembering former emotion.
(Here I insert a parenthesis to point out that I have deliberately dwelt not so much on the incidents which preceded this
scene as on the successive states of mind through which I
passed during these incidents. I have concentrated so meticu-
lously on these with the sole purpose of making that which
is to come more intelligible. I should like to add that I have
little liking for the reconstruction of things remembered.
Neither you nor I are worth taking so seriously or so literally.
Don't you think it's all rather indecent : I made love to so
and so, I was happy, she was unfaithful to me, I was sad, some
fellow threatened me, I was frightened, and so forth? Let me
tell you that it's merely sordid and boring. I know we've got
tongues and we've invented pens, and they're both longing to
be used. But why the dickens do we need tongues and pens?
And in any case, why do we so perversely feel the urge to
chatter inconsiderately in front of a gaping or drowsing audience, and to keep on scribbling in order to compensate for the
inadequacy of our lives? And which of us still have the re-
ticence to indulge in this deplorable habit in private, by themselves? Only maniacs, imbeciles and old bachelors. And note
that I myself don't deny having sought an audience, a very
restricted one indeed but still an audience. All right, then;
don't let us be afraid to talk and write, since we cannot escape
from the common lot.)

The little redheaded man, whose face had assumed a yellow-
ish pallor, hesitated for a while before taking a decision. He
stood waiting with his clenched fists waist-high, ready to hit

out, with a certain air of enjoyment as though he were relishing both the punishment inflicted on him by the young woman, to whose orders he would obviously submit with delight, and his own anger which bore public witness to his love. I felt my blood run cold when I saw his knees shaking under the light grey trousers that hung loosely about his ankles. Until then I had avoided looking him in the face, but now, to master my own fear, I tried to stare at him with a cool, collected look and assumed a nonchalant pose, biting my tongue very hard meanwhile to stop my lips from trembling. And it was with unspeakable relief that I suddenly saw him turn on his heel and, with his head drooping between his narrow sloping shoulders, stagger back to his little table in a corner of the room, from which he could watch us out of the corner of his eye.

This incident closed, I found myself alone with the woman and silence fell between us. While we were dancing, I had already envisaged vaguely the difficulty I should find sooner or later in talking to her in her own language, but I had not really worried about this, particularly as I felt that an exchange of commonplace words might interrupt our ecstasy, and I was glad of the silence to which I was condemned not so much by my customary inability to find any topic of conversation with a stranger as by my ignorance of Spanish, probably equalled by her ignorance of my own tongue. To tell the truth, in my advanced state of intoxication this caused me only a passing uneasiness, and I already caught myself mentally confiding to her certain things about myself which in normal times I should never have considered revealing to my most intimate friend, far less to a person who was prac-

tically unknown to me, even if, feeling strongly attracted and
wishing to make love to her, I had begun to talk about myself
for lack of any better subject.

At this point in my story I realise how difficult it will be to
retrace a particularly obscure and confused incident in my
life, whose incoherent character and whose correct proportions
I ought to reproduce if I want to be truthful, while striving to
avoid tendentiously giving it a significance it never had, or
treating it with an exaggerated detachment which would deprive it, in retrospect, of the emotive value it possessed. The
facts which I am about to relate appeared in so unusual a
light as to justify a mode of narration which, however, I persist in considering dishonest : a certain mistiness, a studied in-
coherence, spell-binding through the impression it would give
of an inverted order of things, a sort of magic obtained by
means of well-timed conjunctions of experience, no matter of
what kind, provided they achieved the effect of verisimilitude,
the complex multiplicity of all those artifices which impress
on the reader's mind the notion of a critical and tense moment
and which would strike him violently enough to do away with
the need of any explanation in logical and discursive language—in short, far more art and far less honesty. Well, no ! I
said at the beginning that I would deny myself the use of such
methods, no doubt effective by that sort of deceitful mirage in
which they drown facts while restoring their original atmosphere of imprecision and disorder, but meanwhile, and this is
the point to which I draw the reader's attention, subjecting
these facts to such distortions that no conclusive interpretation
can possibly be made of them, and this would naturally mean
departing from my aim, which is at the same time more lofty

and more modest. More lofty because I despise those who, under colour of arousing sensibility, wallow in confusion and arbitrariness like ducks in water, and although I notice not without bitterness that falsehood is tolerated, nay, approved of and praised by everyone, yet for my part I intend to cut out scrupulously whatever is not absolutely pure and lucid, today at any rate when I'm in that mood, for after all I don't consider it a duty or a rule of health. More modest, because there is an art of lying which the keenest liars cannot claim to have mastered. Theatrical effects are not my concern, I'd better stick to faithfully describing, as I intend to do here, the successive phases of my attack, preoccupied solely with revealing in broad outline what I witnessed of its evolution. And if you find this boring, that's just too bad.

But first of all I think I must give you a summary notion of the setting, the attitude of the people there towards me, all the subsidiary elements which may have contributed in any way to give rise to an attack which differed from earlier ones not only by its duration, its intensity and its completeness, but also by the unexpected way in which it was transformed into an anguish as keen as had been the pleasure I have tried to describe which was later replaced, in consequence of a violent physical shock, by a delicious daze which, so to speak, brought the curve to a close.

The setting was roughly that of all seaside bars into which you can go on condition of appearing neither too foolish, nor too rich, nor too timid, nor too aggressive, where there are pretty girls dancing with customers and others, less pretty, making eyes at you and sometimes offering you drinks to cheer you up and prove to the *patronne,* as the saucers pile up in

front of you, that you've not come there solely to sit down
and do nothing, where there may be a modest band consisting
of three musicians, worthy fellows but a trifle drunk, each
armed with a different instrument, the first with a saxophone,
the second with an accordion, the third with an upright piano
on which he strums at odd moments when he's tired of staring
over the top of his score at the faces and legs of the women he
fancies, where at a certain moment a gang of half-tipsy sailors
invariably turn up and attract everyone's attention with their
wild talk and gestures, and then one of them, particularly
tough and excited, picks a quarrel with some rustic dandy
who doesn't want to give up his pretty partner, and protests
furiously or tearfully according to the nature of his drunkenness until he gets a sound thrashing and is flung out, with the
timid approval of the management, after being first relieved
of his wallet, and when you leave the place you may also find
your own pockets empty, but usually it's the following afternoon, when you wake up with an iron band round your head
and a mind that's no longer fuddled, that you realise that after
all your evening's outing, which you now refuse to consider
as an evening's pleasure, was not exactly free, gratis and for
nothing. If I don't absolutely give up trying to suggest this
atmosphere, in spite of the somewhat facile romanticism it
inevitably calls up, and although I remain constantly on guard
against any pursuit of the picturesque, it's because I consider
that the setting played its part and I cannot in all fairness pass
it over in silence.

The attitude of people towards me had altered considerably
since my scene with the little redhead; not that this was more
remarkable than most of those witnessed daily in this estab-

lishment; it had had no consequences and had never assumed
that violent character usual in such cases, but that was precisely what made it the more striking in the eyes of the spectators who, knowing from old acquaintance the aggressive
temperament of the man, always ready to make use of his
fists when he considered himself insulted by another's at-
tentions to his girl, were amazed at seeing him yield so readily
to an insignificant-looking stranger, whose pugnacity, to judge
by his negative reactions, must have been of a low order. But
perhaps, too, they thought that my rival, believing me to conceal under a calm indifferent manner a host of wiles unfamiliar to him, had been so keenly impressed that he had
thought it prudent to retreat; at least that was what I chose
to imagine, and to convince myself I let my eye roam round
the room : most of the dancers were watching me with
curiosity, the men openly, the women surreptitiously, and the
way in which both partners of a couple would glance at me
simultaneously while they went on talking, confirmed my
conviction that they were talking about me, and naturally I
felt sure that they were doing so favourably. In any case, one
thing was quite clear : whereas when I entered this dance hall
I had been an obscure and insignificant figure, I now enjoyed
a certain esteem from people who generally respect and admire
only those who are more powerful than themselves, and I
derived from this awareness a disproportionate sense of pride
which probably accounts, in part, for the fact that my attack,
unlike the previous ones, assumed an ostentatious character
the more surprising that I have always detested exhibitionism
in other people. But in company, when I am not preoccupied
with the need for passing unnoticed and seeing without being

seen, I almost invariably try to play a part; usually I should
like to be taken for one of those men from whom you never
know what to expect in the way of reactions, creative work,
attitude towards a given situation and so on, so that each
new contact with them implies a complete change of perspec-
tive; my keenest admiration being for those people whom I can
never quite succeed in classifying, I naturally want to take
them for models. Among a group, particularly if it includes
women, I take acute pleasure in acting my part, not with a
deliberate hypocritical aim but through an instinctive need to
increase my stature and clothe myself with a flattering shadow;
besides, in such a case, what intoxicates me is not so much the
heady savour of deception arising from such play-acting, as
a strange sense of release; I feel as if after a long privation
circumstances had enabled me at last to regain possession of
my birthright, to reassume my own personality. Hence,
despite my horrible memories of life at school and in the
army, I sometimes recall these with a feeling of nostalgia
akin to that of an ageing actress remembering the huge theatre,
resonant with applause, in which she enjoyed her greatest
triumphs.

As for my friends, they could not believe their eyes. My
altercation with the little fellow and the obvious beauty of my
partner altered their opinion of me for a brief while. Not
exactly the insignificant young man who drearily tagged along
behind them! All things considered, I was behaving with
women as they would have liked to do, I represented to some
extent their ideal of what a man ought to be, daring, scornful,
aggressive and sarcastic if the need arose, a little overfond of
drink like all real men, phlegmatic in the face of danger, enter-

prising with women and immediately attractive to them, but above all endowed with superb self-assurance. This, I mean, was what I imagined they were thinking about me. I stood proudly on the pedestal of the successful Don Juan. Indisputably, my present attitude consecrated my manhood, it made up for all my previous failures and, with a last vestige of puerility, I almost took it as a sort of revelation (to myself and to others) of a very general nature, and this made me pass insensibly from the private pleasure of taking people in to the vainglorious desire to show off in public, like an actor who, dizzy with success, overplays his effects because he cannot alter them, and thus gradually reveals their crudity. If I thought carefully, I might perhaps discover other accessory features, of dubious importance, which may have contributed indirectly to provoke that attack, the course of which I can only sketch here, to my great regret. But such investigations would take me too far; and I confess, if I linger too long over the causes, I'm afraid my reader may not follow me as far as the effects. Yes, I must acknowledge that I'm no longer sure of being listened to. I'm losing confidence. It's time, no doubt, it's high time I stopped all this futile beating about the bush, which I myself don't find very enjoyable, and that I gave up once and for all these elaborate manœuvres around the subject when what interests me is the subject itself. I'll plunge straight in. Come back to me, reader, come back, I've finished with the causes and I'm moving on without delay to the description of the event itself.

The two attacks, the first I have described and this one, had only one point in common, that sensation of euphoria which preceded them both; from the actual onset of the attack all resemblance vanishes. It is important to note that they could not have broken out nor developed with such exceptional force had not I myself provided a favourably receptive environment, by being in a very special emotional state induced by circumstances in my private life. In the first case, as we have seen, it was a strange sense of well-being due no doubt to the loneliness of the spot, the cool noise of the waves, the purity of the sky, the delicious shade contrasted with the sight of chalky rocks dazzling white under the sun's inexorable fire and thereby all the more precious, like an oasis in the heart of the desert, together with the no less vivid contrast between the atmosphere of boredom that hung about an afternoon spent in my room and the air which, a little later, I was breathing in at every pore by the seaside. In the second case, which we are considering now, my condition, although greatly intensified, retained its peculiar characteristics : the same optimism, the same ardent yet passive enjoyment, the same detachment, which did not preclude a strong feeling of sympathy for my surroundings; only the causes had changed. I don't want to ignore the possibly important fact that I had consumed a large amount of alcohol, which some people may ironically consider of paramount significance; but nothing will prevent me from believing that the sight of so marvellously beautiful woman was the sole cause of the electrifying pleasure I experienced, just as this in its turn was necessary to prepare a favourable ground for the outbreak of the most violent attack I ever endured. How can I make myself clear? It was impossible to remain silent with those eyes upon one; convinced that one could never confide to anybody else the essential things one had to say, and that if one persisted in keeping silent one would lose one's last chance, one naturally sought to seize an opportunity that would not come again. In the same way, I am naturally inclined today not only to ascribe a leading role to the magical attraction this woman exercised over me, but also to express some doubt as to the importance of the part played by my inebriation, by the noise and bustle of the place and any other factor of that sort, which seem to me secondary and somewhat problematical.

As at the onset of my previous attacks, my elation gave place to a burning desire to speak, but, surprisingly enough, the substitution occurred so naturally, so insidiously that it never entered my mind that here was a fresh manifestation of my disorder; and this was due to the fact that for the first time my desire was promptly satisfied : I had already begun to speak when I became aware of it. The change took place, as it were, without the preliminary consent of my will, so that I did not even have to cope with the agonising and always fruitless efforts with which I usually strove to get free of my obscure burden, and which had hitherto set their dreaded mark on the very memory of my last attacks. Later, however, I was to go through a different hell.

With a singular irresponsibility, which moreover merely emphasises the definitely ostentatious aspect of my attack, I began to talk at the precise moment when the band stopped playing and the lively conversations suddenly flagged. I talked, and it was a magnificent sensation. It seemed to me that by thus displaying what I scarcely dared admit to myself, I was casting off a heavy burden, that I had at last discovered how to free myself from certain restraints which are commonly held necessary for the good of the public, in such a way as to

recover a lightheartedness which I had always sought, but so
far without success; I felt released from that morbid agitation
that one fosters secretly within a closed and forbidden world;
conflicts, fevers, chaos had ceased; I had a day's respite at
least; there reigned within me an ever increasing serenity which
was no longer the fruit of inertia but that of innumerable
earlier efforts which had gone unrewarded till now; I had cast
off the yoke of a man doomed to perpetual solitary confine-
ment, I was gradually pouring it all out, with a delight as overwhelming as the most successful erotic pleasure. Don't accuse
me of deliberate vagueness as to the nature of my admissions;
for one thing I am not concerned here with discussing these;
if you're dying to find out about them, I warn you that you're
going to be sadly disappointed, for with due deference to those
people who assume that an autobiographer is endowed with
an infallible memory and that one is entitled to expect from
him an exact account of all his actions, although I have indeed
promised to study conscientiously and straightforwardly the
complex mechanism of my attacks, I have no intention of relating every detail, including those I have never known. It's
not my fault if the most important part eludes me, indeed has
already eluded me, when it looks as if I ought to have grasped
it so readily. I have already said that on no account would I
distort facts; if some of these are lacking for the understanding of the whole, I'm willing to forgo the advantage I should
gain by making a stronger impression on the reader's mind
with certain fictitious incidents, I will never fill the gaps due to
forgetfulness with plausible falsehoods. If the curious or the
meticulous object, it can't be helped; I would rather lay myself open to the unjustified charge of keeping silent about

admissions which might compromise me—though I can scarcely believe that anyone is still naïve enough to imagine I am bothered about compromising myself. It matters little to me that by omission, or out of genuine forgetfulness, I may have cast a shadow of doubt over what, in its general lines, is so obviously authentic. But how comes it, I hear you ask, that I have forgotten precisely the most significant, or at least the most intriguing part of my story? To this I have nothing to reply. And yet I could perhaps provide an explanation which would satisfy fair-minded people. Deplorable and unlikely as the fact may be from certain angles, I have completely forgotten what disclosures I made, for the simple reason that while I was making them I paid no attention to them. I will make this clear. The vital thing for me was to talk, irrespective of what I was talking about. Obsessed by delight at my release I scarcely noticed the appalling things I was saying and was only aware of them through their reflection on the faces of my audience, alternately alight with ardent curiosity, distorted with disgust or white with indignation, like members of a jury listening to a prisoner who is somewhat too communicative for a man supposedly overwhelmed with remorse, but whose self-mastery is complete, calmly relating the unspeakable crimes that have brought him in front of them. In other words, even if I thought that this is not the place to confide in strangers certain intimate details which were only revealed in public under the influence of an attack of illness, even if legitimate shame deterred me from revealing once again secrets which I have always regretted betraying, I should be quite incapable of satisfying my readers' curiosity and, as I have said, I have firmly resolved not to yield, and to disregard

the incredulity of these same suspicious, disappointed readers;
they won't succeed in making me add one word of my own
invention.

The woman sat in silence watching me hold forth, with a
frown on her brow, her elbows on the table and her little fists
pressed against her temples. She never took her eyes off me,
even when she suddenly grasped her glass and raised it greedily
to her lips as if, shocked and fascinated by my revelations,
whose sordidness I deliberately exaggerated out of bravado,
she sought Dutch courage to help her endure their savage tone.
Not once did I see her turn her eyes away; she was watching
my lips, bending slightly forward and leaning her head on her
right fist, from which drifted up the blue smoke of her cigarette which she held carefully between finger and thumb;
she was motionless, sitting stiffly in strange inaction, in an
attitude of rest which was rather that of exhausting tension. I
think I cannot have spoken for quite as long as I imagined;
time had ceased to exist, or rather I was outside time, for in
my urgent need to unburden myself completely before I was
forced to be silent, I spoke faster and faster, with increasing
effrontery, in a dizzy rush that lifted me out of time, facing
without fear or shame the storm of anger I felt rising amongst
the crowd of spectators, who had begun to close in round us.
I mean that the world of human preoccupations was suddenly
suspended, lulled asleep as it were; a marvellous armistice had
been concluded, time was annihilated, all links with external
things abolished.

And yet the delight I experienced at exhibiting myself in
public gave place, little by little, to terror at the distress suddenly revealed on the woman's face, and the sounds of low

muttering and whistling, expressive of growing disapproval, uttered by the excited crowd behind her as they argued in eager whispers and sometimes pointed accusing fingers at me. The air was heavy with disaster; things were not going as well as they had seemed to a few moments earlier, but as I have said, the tense dramatic atmosphere that now pervaded the whole room, instead of paralysing me, impelled me on the contrary to defy my audience by adding some even more sordid touch to my already shocking revelations. I have said, too, that I was not immune from the pleasure—extravagant, but much sought after by certain men who are concerned to make an impression—of provoking interest by all possible effects, even the least honourable, and when curiosity flags, whetting it anew by going a little further, then much further than the most elementary decency could allow. I don't think my verdict can be imputed to excessive self-analysis when I assert that the feelings of curiosity, repulsion and finally of hostility which my attitude so obviously aroused satisfied my longing for display in proportion to their violence; I could with all lucidity of mind indulge in the seductive conviction that I was that evening (whether as hero, butt or common foe) the focus of all eyes, from those of the pretty girl who listened to me with an attentiveness that was all the more constant and scrupulous, so I thought, because my utterance was too rapid for her imperfect knowledge of the French language, to the angrily glittering eyes of the other men and women—not, presumably, the sort of people to be easily astonished. And yet, despite the ecstatic effect of such a verbal erection—my whole body was in a trance, my throat seemed on fire—and the positive but more ordinary pleasure I enjoyed from being the centre of interest, it cannot be denied that I was afraid. Perhaps this is not quite correct. Perhaps I was not afraid. When I say I was afraid I mean I was perfectly aware that I was sliding down a dangerous slope and, without ascribing to this image more than an evocative value, that I would touch the bottom of the abyss, whatever efforts I might make to check my fall and to climb up again. It was a fear akin to that which I indulged in when, barely out of childhood, I travelled through a wood by night and deliberately imagined wolves, murderers and ghosts waiting for me in the darkness, and when my heart was sufficiently numb with terror I experienced a sort of intoxicating satisfaction at the thought that it lay as much in my power to make my heart throb and my nerves quiver as to raise my little finger, or to dispose of my soul. If you had seen the provocative glances cast by certain young pimps, disconcerted by the blend of subtlety and intolerable indecency in my remarks, by which they felt personally insulted, as if I had spat in their faces (they were clearly longing for an opportunity to fling me out unceremoniously), if you had seen the sneers of their girl friends who, avid for sensation, delightedly sniffing a scandal but failing to understand its nature, assumed an attitude of mingled irony and contempt, without feeling any natural impulse to mock or despise me, if above all you had seen those eyes of dazzling brilliance, with their silvery glitter, in that serious watchful face, and those deep red lips thickened by a trace of negro blood, giving a livid hue to the white skin, I think that in that case, with all due respect to those who claim never to let themselves be led astray by uncontrollable emotions, if you had been in a parallel situation, that's to say inspired by the same strange need to talk, wounded and spurred on by the general hostility yet passionately desirous of conquering a certain woman, even at the cost of your reputation, you would have experienced an agitation like that to which I was a prey, an agitation whose constituent elements (which I shall never succeed in exhausting by analysis) were paradoxically anguish, feverish excitement, ecstasy, naïve pride, satisfied vanity, desire—and, had you tried to do so, you could not have mastered it better than I.

And then, at the very moment when, ignoring the stupid blindness of the rest, I was musing without mental reservations on all the secret affinities between this woman and myself, when I was feeling happy at finding her silent, grave, attentive, although apparently slow to probe the meaning of some of my admissions on account of her evident incapacity to follow all the terms of an unfamiliar language, which in any case excused me from watching my words too closely and from leaving unmentioned certain details which disclosed rather too much and might thus prejudice the favourable impression I hoped she had of me, but which despite their shockingly intimate nature I was impelled to reveal by the fear of breaking the thread of my discourse, at the very moment when, sincerely convinced that an element of genuine emotion had at last entered into my life in the shape of this lovely foreigner, and that our complicity was about to assume—had already begun to assume, with extraordinary intensity—the character of a crucial experience, everything was leading me to believe that I had at last succeeded in exchanging my cold unhappy solitude (which actually was for the most part neither cold nor unhappy but only seemed so by contrast with my desire) for the heartening warmth of mutual understanding—at that very

D

moment, it shames me to say so, this woman, who was after all only a tart like all the rest, broke into loud laughter in my face.

II

I staggered hurriedly to the door, but before opening it I looked back. She was still sitting there convulsed with laughter, tears pouring down her cheeks, the dance-hall customers were thronging round her in a ring, screaming with laughter themselves, leaning sideways with hand on hip and stomach thrust forward, delighted, presumably, at being released from the silence to which my long speech had relegated them and able to give free rein to their exasperation, which in fact found expression in a frenzied hilarity interrupted by shrill yelps and thigh-slappings. The sight was nauseating! As soon as I had shut the door behind me the whole hall rang with a staccato chatter of voices like machine-gun fire. In the street I felt at first relieved to have left that over-heated noisy room. The snow had hardened and the air was colder. A cold that penetrated one's clothes and into the very pores of one's skin, dilated with alcohol, and stole into one's bones. The streets were empty, the lamps sparse and distant. Thrusting my hands deep in my pockets against the cold, with my collar turned up and buttoned under my chin, I crept along the walls, peering cautiously around me and taking care to look back from time to time to make sure I was not being followed. A white line ran down the middle of the empty road, dwindling into the distance, over the pallid icy surface of the asphalt streaked with patches of snow. Laughter and shouts reached me, remote, muffled by the foggy air, in a close weft of sound underlined by the blare of the band, which had begun to play again. Gasping in the cold air, I paused a moment to get my breath, and cast a glance of relief down the street, on one side of which stood, at the place where I had stopped, a long low building whose façade consisted merely of a white wall with one huge double door standing wide open, ensconced at the end of a fenced-in garden which winter had transformed into a snowy steppe, and on the other side a series of small houses which had nothing remarkable about them except the fact that they were all built of stone and that all their windows were provided with iron balconies whose strictly identical arabesques were clearly defined against the thin layers of snow spread everywhere. Much farther off, in front of me, glittered the voluminous, intensely white mass of the first trees in the public gardens, in which the great firtree which for thirty years had been its principal ornament rose upright like a mountain peak. The whole of this frozen, abstract landscape, the gleaming austerity of these buildings sharply outlined against the snow, the muffled and as it were sterilised atmosphere, the emptiness of these clean, straight streets which seemed to belong to some deserted city, even that great doorway open on an equally deserted courtyard, displayed that inhuman character which, wherever revealed, has always thrilled me, and perhaps I responded the more keenly to its blend of severity and velvet-softness, to its geometrical and yet miraculous quality, because it contrasted so sharply with the disorderly atmosphere of the low tavern I had just left; without seeking any deeper meaning in the coincidence, I cannot resist noting how exactly this contrast corresponded with two tendencies in my nature, be-

tween which I wavered continually and which sometimes
seemed to me to control between them every aspect of my
emotional life : suddenly feeling an insurmountable repug-
nance for social life with its train of intrigues, its contemptible
agitation and its hollow talk, for the stifling warmth emanating
from a promiscuity to which life's sinister obligations condemned me, I would strive to escape from it all and enjoy the
benefits of silence and a purer air, but no sooner had I yielded
to this impulse than, terrified by the prospect of being henceforward cut off from any human contact, and justified by this
fear, in my own eyes, in deserting a position which I still maintain to be the better one, I would hasten to wallow delightedly
in the cesspool of social life, although soon, unable to find
rational satisfaction there and convinced once more that my
life was incompatible with that of others, I fled from it precipitately, shaking off its dirt, to shelter once again in that
inviolable spot of which I had dreamed, and so it went on.
This state of perpetual alternation was highly painful, but at
the present moment I had not yet reached the stage of dis-
satisfaction; the memory of that stuffy smoke-filled room, the
glaring light on the close-packed crowd of dancers, the vulgar
laugh of that woman which now seemed a betrayal of our
tacit agreement, the whole atmosphere of popular revelry
which had delighted me a short while ago only made keener
the pleasure I now took in contemplating that still, silent,
frozen landscape where I stood alone.

And yet, while I made my way down a narrow lane where
the north wind whistled round my ears, I was desperately
trying to recall how that woman had smiled while we were
dancing together; generally I find no difficulty in remembering

just as much as I want of a sight that has given me pleasure, for instance of a face that has impressed me in the street, and often as I lie awake at night I can recall it in every detail with remarkable precision until I grow weary of this analysis and press on to something else, but this time, even at the cost of extreme efforts, I could find no trace of that smile whose attraction for me I have already described. It was exasperating; I wanted to remember it, I passionately wanted to remember it, the more so because I was reluctant to admit this longing to myself, and I tried at first to recollect her hair, what sort of jewels hung in her ears and the curious way she narrowed her eyes as she looked at me, and what her nose was like. And so, little by little and as it were casually I drew nearer to the vital spot, but just as I thought I'd got hold of that smile a horrible burst of laughter flooded into my memory. And then I had to begin stalking that smile all over again with ever greater prudence and cunning, until repeated failure made me finally abandon the attempt. On the other hand, that laughter was perfectly clear, only too clear, and it seemed indeed as if the recollection of it would stay with me until death or beyond.

Enough of that! I am lying! I was lying when I held forth so solemnly about the feelings of relief I experienced on beholding that cold silent landscape; to speak truth at last, I took no more interest in it than in remembering that woman, who had irremediably lost in my eyes all the charm and glamour due, to a large extent, to her enigmatic smile. I was lying; I'm sorry to say my feelings were very far from serene, and when I had just been subjected, under the circumstances

I have described, to an insult which had wounded me more
than if someone had spat in my face, how could I have attached the slightest importance to the icy purity of that street
down which I hurried, hugging the wall like a creature in disgrace? I was not even trying to shake off that despair mingled
with self-contempt into which I had been cast by that burst of
laughter which I perversely delighted in remembering, with
a curious persistence due no doubt to the imperious attraction
its remembrance exercised on my mind, and tormented as I
was by a dual feeling of guilt and of more or less admitted
disgrace, I longed above all for the extreme fulfilment of a
curse from which I derived a sort of enjoyment like that of a
penitent who not only accepts his just chastisement as natural
but indeed demands it with a fervour corresponding to his
wish to expiate. The fact is that I was inclined to consider
this laugh as a punishment for having too complacently indulged in confidences for which, however great was the relief
I experienced at the time, I was going to have to pay a heavy
price. Now I shall doubtless be expected to provide a plausible
explanation of this lie, at any rate by those who, anxious to see
me inveigled into a second lie, ironically urge me to justify
myself. They may be greatly surprised and, who knows? possibly flattered if I admit that I have tried to mislead them by
ascribing to myself such unexceptionable thoughts, less from
fear of the shame I might have felt on recalling that laugh
which had cut me like a knife, than because I had reason
to fear their own laughter, yes, your laughter, gentlemen! I
have to make a declaration which is eminently comical, or
which will undoubtedly be considered such by certain ill-
intentioned folk. I feel obliged therefore to forestall them by

pointing out that I'm no good at joking, I have absolutely no
aptitude for playing the fool, as everyone must realise except
those who are given to laughing at what they don't understand very well, in other words who find highly amusing what
is really rather sad, whereas people of another sort shed tears
over something that they might well laugh at. Without being
sure which category I am addressing, I think in any case that
I'm not asking too much from either of them when I beg them
to display the utmost gravity, complete impassibility, which
doesn't imply entire comprehension, or at any rate a disdainful
silence accompanied—I've no objection to that—by a majestic
shrug of the shoulders, in a word, shall I be understood if I
say that what I need is not so much complicity, approval,
respect or interest as silence? Ah, silence! Shall I be believed,
then, if I have the face to proclaim here my insurmountable
aversion to people who have a mania for confession? This is
sure to delight a number of poor creatures who are trying
surreptitiously to convict me of inconsistency, and confuse a
few innocents who from reading the preceding pages conscientiously, if not very attentively, are inclined to think the opposite, and I can just hear them seizing the opportunity to ask
me, the former with an ironical smile and the latter flinging
up their arms in despair, what else I think I've been doing all
this while? Far from being put off by the insolent nature of
such a question, I propose to answer it presently if I have time,
but supposing I am urged to give an immediate reply I shall
first point out to those who boast of having caught me out in
a glaring contradiction that they would be committing a grave
error, not to say a grave injustice, if they refused to take into
account an affliction which is peculiar to myself and whose

various symptoms I propose to submit to them here. As for the
rest, I'll return to it in due course.

One of the reasons for my sense of shame lay precisely in
the repulsion I had always felt for those who yield to the
temptation of disclosing their inmost thoughts, either for the
morbid pleasure of casting off an inward discipline which is,
to my mind, essential to human honour and in any case for
mental health, or else to obtain temporary relief from some
obsession, or else for the ignoble delight of self-humiliation
before one of their fellow-men. Herein, perhaps, lies the true
cause of that inability to confide in anyone which, as I said
earlier, had so much hindered the intimate relations I should
have liked to have with my friends. For me, to confide in any
degree or to serve as confidant in order to oblige somebody
else is equal to selling one's soul to the devil in exchange for a
few years' prosperity; how vain, indeed, is the pleasure which
is paid for by an eternity of suffering! In what is grandly
called confession I see nothing but the reprehensible and highly
costly indulgence in a vice, and I shall always look with the
greatest suspicion on any friendship in which each party is
continually engaged in worming precious secrets out of the
other. Whenever I have witnessed the all-too-common spectacle
of two men with flushed faces leaning towards each other, with
looks of heartfelt interest and tender smiles, across a table
stacked with empty bottles and the congealing remains of a
substantial meal (just see how they play at feeling themselves
understood and, excited by food and good wine, with what
ingenuous shamelessness they unburden themselves to one
another, indulging in it to their hearts' content, and what an
inward glow of happiness is revealed on their radiant faces),

whenever I have happened to pass a confessional where, amid propitious gloom, the voices of priest and penitent are heard muttering alternately, endlessly whispered questions and answers, I have invariably felt a sort of uneasiness or even a fierce anger which, swift as a whirlwind, rose inexplicably into my head; I have noticed that the sight of such contemptible practices, although justified by the approval of some and the indifference of others, never failed to arouse in me a violent disgust or, if I myself had unfortunately been involved, an intolerable sense of my own degradation. To judge by the burst of laughter with which that woman had greeted my outpourings the sight of such shamelessness may presumably arouse in other people feelings of less violent hostility which are none the less quite as cruelly wounding to their object. After all, to see a man behave like that in public may perhaps be ludicrous as well as distressing? She had not shrunk from me in disgust as I am sure I should have done in her place : she had burst out laughing. A vulgar laugh, by which she openly proclaimed her treachery, if indeed she had not been in my enemies' camp all along while acting so as to confirm my belief that our two destinies had by some miracle come together and that I should always find in her a sure and loyal ally, miming all the signs of complicity and thus deceiving me about her true intentions, the more easily because of her natural seductiveness, all this in order to win my confidence and provoke me to persist in my comic role, unless she was simply hoping to get from me what a woman of that sort usually wants. In any case it was unquestionably the memory of that laugh, and not that of the threatening attitudes more or less openly adopted by my other hearers, that disclosed to me in a decisive flash the degrading

and ridiculous element in my behaviour; it alone served to
arouse in me an almost physical sense of humiliation and to
bring me at last full awareness of what could only be considered a sort of disgrace which I should never be able to forget nor to recover from, whatever mental efforts I made to
rehabilitate myself in my own eyes. And I felt justified in considering this laugh as a well-deserved penalty for having exposed myself in public with remarks which I now reproached
myself with secret vehemence for having uttered before so
large and ill-chosen an audience. Shall I now be told that this
is an utterly extravagant interpretation? Have I not myself
admitted that I was not in full possession of my faculties : why
persist in describing and discussing utterly commonplace
events to which an unprejudiced mind would refuse to ascribe
any importance? Finally, is not that sense of abjectness
identical with that experienced by many drunkards, and what
is its connection with my attack of garrulousness? I am obviously trying to show off and making strenuous efforts to
provide causes too unusual to be insignificant for perfectly
insignificant results. Either I am refusing, out of pride, to admit that I was drunk, that this state of drunkenness induced
me to tell my secrets and that consequently there was something grotesque in my attitude at which nobody could help
laughing, or else I am once again the victim of a sensory
illusion. In short, people would like to force me to admit that
my ecstasy, my urge to talk and the shame that ensued are all
to be accounted for by my inebriation and are, in the last
analysis, merely varied aspects of this. Never under any pre-
text will I accept this point of view. Although I have already
stressed the excited state I was in through having drunk a fair

amount of alcohol, I insist and I shall maintain at all costs
that it would be absurd to exaggerate the importance of this,
that my remarks were in no wise those of a drunkard and
that there was nothing incoherent about them which might
raise a laugh or even a smile. My unshakable opinion is that
however strongly a man may be tempted to unburden his
heart he must never forget that, in so far as he oversteps the
limits of decent reserve, he lays himself open to irony on the
one hand, to anger on the other. I, for my part, had been
cruelly shattered by irony.

Meanwhile, after walking the whole length of the narrow
lane that leads to the canal, I turned off down a neighbouring
street, looking behind me constantly, although it seemed highly
unlikely that anyone would follow me. I made a half-hearted
show of examining the rare shop windows whose shutters were
not drawn down, and these halts enabled me to keep furtive
watch over the street corners, where I vaguely expected to
see a shadow cast on the snowy road or on the walls, plastered
here and there with torn posters on which the gas lamps
splashed yellow light. Then I started off again and crossed
the market place, which winter had transformed into a sort
of waste land, a great empty space, closed in at the far end
by lifeless buildings whose stone assumed an aspect of bravado
by the side of the smoky tumbledown backs of several wooden
huts, in which a few humble and often anonymous traders
carried on their business. Around the fresh heaps of dung, reek-
ing of ammonia, which lay between the tracks of horses'
hooves, showing up with obscene precision against the snow,
flocks of crows whirled and swooped with a noise like the
creaking of rusty shutters. In the whole of that forlorn de-

nuded space there was nothing to suggest the confusion of
market days, when the whole countryside foregathered there
to argue and shout and gesticulate. I breathed in with delight
the calm, icy air that set my nostrils tingling and seared my
lungs with its life-giving sharpness. It was only a few steps
further on, when I was roughly on a level with a majestic
statue standing at the end of a great tree-lined boulevard, lifeless and deserted like all the rest, and leading into an area full
of derelict buildings, that I felt certain this time of being followed. I turned round sharply and threw a rapid furtive glance
along the street. I saw nothing unusual save a flurry of snow
raised by a sudden gust of wind, and a few old papers twisting and tumbling along, scraps of newspaper such as lie strewn
about city pavements at dawn. Above me the telegraph wires
emitted an uninterrupted, shrill, strange hum as if the coldness
of the air had found a voice. I started off again, walking
faster, but before I had taken twenty steps I fancied I heard
once more behind me the low sound of hoarse breathing,
rhythmically accompanying my footsteps; instead of halting
and turning round as I had done before, I began to run as fast
as I could along the middle of the boulevard, panting and
gasping, until breathlessness and a stitch in my side forced me
to slow down considerably and then to stop altogether. After
a moment I caught the sound of hurrying steps which could
not have been more than fifty yards behind. I swung round
with a promptness which might have seemed like a nervous
reflex, but could see no human being, no suspicious shadow,
except just at the edge of the darkness, some thirty yards away,
a handcart which stood abandoned by the pavement with its
two handles raised towards the misty heavens, motionless in

the night air which was shimmering with frost like a sheet of glass and where the gas lamps flung trails of sulphurous light. I should find it quite impossible to analyse the mournful impression made on me by this solitary handcart, whose handles outstretched towards an invisible sky in an attitude of entreaty suggested my own distress to me, although at the time I was not conscious of the parallel; in any case the sight struck terror into my heart and inspired a frantic impulse to run straight ahead, hurling myself through the moving barrier of darkness. I had seldom behaved in so absurd a fashion. However, I brought myself to resume my journey at a reasonable pace, merely striding out faster without turning round. I am equally unable to justify the painful impression made on me by the rhythmical sound of the bells that began to ring in the darkness over my head while I was passing round the church, which rose above the neighbouring houses in all the conventional and rigid majesty of a public building; the sounds rose into the frosty air, dissolved into echoes and drifted back forlornly as if they had become the very voice of my distress, a grave and heart-rending voice, a fierce and yet nostalgic voice. But no doubt my disquiet was enhanced by the fact that the prolonged, continuous vibration of the bells made it impossible for me to listen for the light sound of footsteps and the breathing of my invisible follower. I hurried away as fast as I could from this church, whose square mass, bleak and even hostile, added to the frankly repellent impression I had of this district. I even remember the strange irritation I felt at seeing a flock of crows busily cawing over a pile of refuse. I went so far as to fling stones at them, but, startled by my mere gesture, they rose in a mass and dropped down again heavily a little further on. I began to run fast, painfully gasping for breath, the alcohol tossing about in my inwards like a heavy burning stone, and at the foot of the rise, at the end of the boulevard, I turned off along a narrow street between houses with balconies and gloomy façades standing back a little on bare patches of ground planted with a few sparse, dejected trees, the whole landscape gradually emerging from darkness, looking sinister and absurd like some bad photograph. The street opened into another, wider street, lined with a double row of trees and leading, on the right, into the public garden. When I entered the latter I had the feeling that this was the place to which my steps must inevitably have led me, although I had no reason to venture hither rather than elsewhere; everything had happened as if I had been the victim of a cunning plot laid by my anonymous pursuer who, being perfectly familiar with the town's topography, had driven me through a maze of lanes and squares only to bring me unawares and unexpectedly into this place. It was a triangular peninsula surrounded by water and joined to the land by a single bridge serving as entrance and exit, and undoubtedly formed the perfect trap where my enemy could corner me. I went on nonetheless along the ridged walk which led into a hollowed-out circus with a pseudo-Greek balustrade, above which towered a gigantic fir-tree visible from all over the town, while deserted stone seats formed a semicircle around a thick carpet of snow which, in spring, would melt to disclose a pavement of shining red gravel. I sat down on a seat at the foot of the fir-tree, first sweeping the snow off it with a dead branch. Strangely enough it was only then that I experienced a real sense of relief and security. I had no thought now of casting anxious glances around me, I

suddenly stopped being afraid; afraid of what? was I even
sure of my enemy's existence? He might quite well have been
a figment of my imagination, which excessive drinking had
made particularly lively, while, seized by unreasoning panic
and haunted by the notion of an irremissible punishment to
which, in my terror, I gave a human form, I had fled so wildly
only in a desperate attempt to escape him. And now that I was
released from this obsession and that things no longer appeared
in a tragic light, nothing prevented me from quietly enjoying
the beauty of a spot where I no longer felt hunted nor threatened, and on which memories of bygone springs conferred an
overwhelming magic power. For this was the very seat on
which I loved to sit in the springtime when the garden was as
thickly swarming with noisy children and embracing couples,
as clamorous with the chirpings and cries of birds, their reson-
ance strangely enhanced by the surrounding water, as glittering with sunlight and green shadow as it was, today, deserted,
silent and black. I liked this moated garden because of the
somewhat rowdy spectacle of children at play and also, I am
ashamed to confess, because of the saturnine pleasure I took
in teasing the few girls who sat there by themselves, and who at
first submitted willingly to my insistent scrutiny as being a
necessary preliminary, but in the end, irritated by what they
took perhaps for shyness, gave up making eyes at me or showing
their legs and even sometimes left their seat abruptly, cheeks
flushed with anger, and hurried back into the streets, either
because they had guessed my tricks or because my passivity
had discouraged them for good. But this garden, even empty
of its inmates, could bind me with its own spell: a triangle of
sand and greenery, with its apex like a ship's prow cleaving

the waters, it gave me the feeling of being at the end of the earth, and from this seat I could watch not only the torrent below me, tumbling in luminous transparent coils from the top of the weir down to a huge foaming whiteness on a bed of pebbles, but also the whole long prospect of the river spanned by so many bridges that even when visibility was perfect you could not count them all, and finally beyond the stream that great compact impenetrable wall, crested with lime-trees, which intrigued me because of the mysterious hubbub to be heard there at certain hours of the day, made up of footsteps running or walking over gravel and excited voices of children at play to which the shrill tinkle of a bell put an abrupt stop. But what I wish I could express was the sensuous pleasure, peaceful and yet extremely acute, that I felt when, sitting motionless on this seat from which I could command the view of a landscape composed of water, buildings and greenery as far as the eye could see, of clouds touched with magic brightness by the spring light, my body warmed by the mild sunshine and protected by a thickish coat from the wind, which was still cool at that time of year, I sat there a long time staring alternately at the people walking to and fro in front of me, at the gleaming steel bridge that spanned the weir or else, raising my head, at the light green vault of the fir-tree looking down on me from its great height, all quite ordinary things in themselves, and meanwhile listening to the random chatter of the people sitting by me, the merry shouts of the children, the rushing murmur of the water tumbling down under the metal bridge; the twofold action of looking and listening had long been bound up for me with a very special emotion that was liable to arise at the most unexpected moment and to be caused by something or someone of no special interest to me. Doing nothing at all, amidst the vast flux of things, but looking and listening. If anyone at such a time had tried to rouse me from the ecstasy induced by such contemplation, I might have reacted violently out of self-defence and replied to the most harmless questions with insulting words or gestures, for which I should later feel sorry and apologise. But it so happens that I have never had occasion to repel any unwelcome interruption, since I go unnoticed everywhere. (The pleasant counterpart to my insignificant appearance, of which I am forever complaining, is this free and heedless way of life.)

Believe me, it's not from complacency that I have dwelt at such length on a period in my life which this garden seat recalled to my mind, but in the first place to point out that, whatever those people may say who seek happiness without ever finding it, happiness is shining in front of their eyes and ringing in their ears at every moment of the day, and they should snatch it wherever it lies, however briefly, and cease wearying us with their futile lamentations; in the second place, to show the importance I attach to the connection between the abrupt disappearance of my terror and the memories of quiet bliss irresistibly evoked for me by the sight of that garden bench on which I had just sat down. It is very striking, indeed, that I should have ceased to believe in the reality of my peril from the moment I set foot in the garden. This phenomenon interests me as a symptom of the influence that such memories, provided they retain something of their violent savour, can have even on a mind dominated by fear, as mine was. But enough of that.

One further remark. I forgot to point out another fact

E

which also strikes me as significant, and I cannot bring myself to pass it over in silence, despite my constant intention to deal only with essentials. It will have been noticed that from the moment I became aware of the danger from which I was trying to escape by rushing through the streets, there was no longer any question of that painful sense of guilt caused, as I think I have fully explained, by the recollection of my contemptible behaviour in the bar and made more acute by the memory of that woman's laughter. The fact is that this sense of guilt disappeared of itself when fear overtook me, and it is equally remarkable that it failed to reassert its sway when, on the threshold of the public garden, fear vanished in its turn; but this time I was entirely possessed by the fascinating music of my memories, nothing could have impaired my delight; I was scarcely conscious of the present. And yet how long should I be subject to the power of that same music? would not it, too, be dispelled eventually, leaving me once again to expiate by cruel self-disgust the shame of having talked in public? And in fact everything took place in the way I have suggested, but this time, so oppressive was my sense of disgrace that, considering fear to be the surest remedy, convinced that fear alone would allow me to experience a certain relief, if not to escape entirely from the grip of remorse, I reached the point of wishing fear back, and of longing for the ordeal of some punishment from which I was sure I would emerge regenerate.

The moon rose, I gave a start : the gate had just closed with a light shrill creak, somebody had come into the garden. I raised myself a little on my hands and looked beyond the snow-coated shrubbery to see if anything was coming round the bend of the path : the bridge was empty, save for two barrels of tar stacked one on the other and a heap of paving-stones surmounted by a red flag waving gently in the wind. I smelt the ice-cold, subtle odour of the water, I could hear the rushing stream, and now the bridge showed clearly, with its stiff gleaming lines, in the moon-dappled semi-darkness. I shook myself, I think I began to laugh; I drew out my hand-kerchief to wipe the sweat that was beading on my forehead. For the moment I was still quite self-possessed, for the moment I still wanted to enjoy the slow exaltation of this sleepless night, to feel time slipping through my fingers and to reject anything that might involve me in too much expenditure of energy and therefore to keep my attention perfectly disengaged. And yet I could not help staring fixedly first at the bridge and then at the path which, between the round patches of light of the gas-lamps, led off into the darkness.

A deep throaty cough startled me. My fingers tightened nervously on the bench and I glanced all round me with a sort of strenuous eagerness. I was about to rise and make my escape when I caught sight of a shadow close to the shrubbery : a few yards away from me, barring my way on the other side of the path, a man was moving slowly, with one hand in his jacket pocket and his hat pulled down over one eye; but instead of coming towards me he crossed the lawn and went in under the lime-trees until I could no longer discern him from where I sat. But he turned on his heel immediately, retraced his steps, crossed the lawn again with stealthy steps and stopped when he reached the shrubbery, hiding behind a tree. To my own amazement I stepped towards him with my elbows slightly raised in the aggressive posture of a wrestler about to grapple, while the moonlight streamed over my shoulders like white

water. Whereas I am usually incapable of performing any
daring action, or even of behaving coolly in face of an enemy
whose strength is greater than or merely equal to my own, this
time I went boldly to meet real danger, as though, released
from any fear or at any rate making it a point of honour to
overcome it, I felt myself equal to tackling an adversary of
whose very name I was ignorant, whereas prudence would
have advised me to sit quietly on my bench, where I was sure
he could not see me. (My unremitting dread of being taken
in now foils the plot by which hypocrisy and vanity would
have induced me to mistake myself for someone so unlikely as
a hero. Moreover, to seek comfort in self-approval, whether deserved or not, strikes me as vulgar, and not permissible under
any circumstances. There's no use my defending myself for
having tried to explain such audacious behaviour by a courage
in which I have already said I was totally lacking. Make no
mistake about it, I was moved by a wish to have done with
the threat of punishment that obsessed me; I dreamed of ex-
piating, by the chastisement I was about to incur, the shame
of my recent conduct and, when my debt was paid, of freely
enjoying a present unadulterated by remorse; the presence of
an enemy seemed a rare opportunity of which advantage must
be taken, in contempt of fear, and by paying for my redemption at the cost of physical suffering. It was thus not with a
fighter's pride, nor with any longing for victory, mastery or
glory that I went to face him, but with the passive humility
of a willing victim who finds it natural and desirable to incur
the punishment he knows he has deserved; I had not got to
conquer an adversary, I had to accept the blows of a man who
seemed to me the chosen instrument to purify me of my taint

and towards whom I should therefore harbour only grateful feelings.) When I was a few yards from him I slowed down, then halted in front of a recently felled tree that blocked the way, at the point where the path from the bridge joined the main alley I had just left, with my eyes fixed on the man, who stood leaning motionless against the tree-trunk, clutching round him a long coat that flapped about his legs. For one moment I fancied we were watching one another, but when he suddenly sprang away from the tree and poked his head forward to stare at me with stupefied amazement I realised that he had only just discovered me. While he was examining me with his sharp little eyes, my whole body, tense with anguish and indecision, quivered with a slight rocking movement. The man's shadow, spread across the whole of the snowy field behind him so that the shadow of his head, now turned sideways over his shoulder and grotesquely distorted by the unevenness of the ground, reached the bridge, and this gave him a gigantic and threatening appearance which he was far from possessing in reality, since he was short and somewhat puny in build. I saw him open his coat and draw out a watch; he looked at the time, raised his head and, watch in hand, took a step towards me, staring me angrily in the eyes; a moment later he looked down at the watch again and replaced it carefully in his waistcoat pocket, then with numb fingers tried to fasten his coat again. It was not until he suddenly pushed back his hat, disclosing a triangle of greasy red hair, that I recognised my little rival from the bar. Poor wretch, hadn't he understood that I was quite indifferent now to his girl friend's charms, hadn't he seen her hold me up to ridicule in front of all the company in the dance hall? I felt very sorry for him

and resolved more strongly than ever to let him beat me to his
heart's content. In the darkness I could not clearly see his face,
but I imagined it must be pale and distorted by hatred, not
very pleasant to see. Poor wretch! He thought no doubt that
by flogging me he would gain the victory for his love, and
meanwhile he was revelling in his rage. There's real passion
for you! Give your neighbour a thrashing for love of your lady.
A noble ideal! The fellow had all my sympathy, I was glad
fate had sent him to me at such a moment, when it almost
seemed as if he had come in answer to my need for expiation,
rather than guided by hatred, to offer himself as executioner. I
liked to think that there had been between us, from our first
contact, a sort of complicity born of our common yearning. He
wanted to beat me just as much as I wanted to be beaten, so
each of us would satisfy a natural need in his own way. No,
his face could not be ugly or gloomy, it must rather have worn
the blissful look of a man who sees a longed-for object within
his reach.

    The moon, which had been hidden for a moment, emerged
in a rent in the clouds and flooded us with icy light. Without
seeming to move his bloodshot eyes he looked me up and down,
with his features set in an expression of mingled resentment
and fear, both hands thrust deep in his coat pockets and im-
perceptibly twitching the stuff. He drew out his right slowly
and then thrust it between the two lapels of his coat, pulled
out his watch and consulted it again with a circumspect air. He
suddenly flung back his head and gave me a long look, sharp
and mistrustful, as if he had good reason to think I should
take advantage of a moment's inattention to make my escape.
Then he leapt over the fallen tree and in two strides covered

the distance between us; his outthrust arm was about to catch
me round the body and throw me backwards, when I dived
sideways and dodged it. I don't think this first attempt to
avoid suffering was due to incurable cowardice, nor was it a
cunning defensive move intended to enable me to take advantage of the bewilderment caused to my adversary by so inane
a gesture, the proof being that I made no attempt to follow
it up; presumably taken by surprise by the rapidity of his
attack, and having thus had neither time nor presence of mind
to control my self-protective reflex, I had instinctively dodged
the blow, thus sharply contradicting my own intentions.

But when he leapt at me once more I merely raised my
elbow to protect my eyes, and he had no difficulty in landing
his fist on the corner of my mouth, which began to bleed profusely. Resolved to yield neither to fear nor to such pride as
was left me until I had endured to the end the ordeal which
was to seal my redemption, I strove with frenzied diligence
to keep my arms close to my sides, in the somewhat ludicrous
attitude of a defenceless victim in the hands of a cruel tor-
turer. But, irritated by the inertia I displayed, the little fellow
drew himself up to his full height and dealt me a great blow on
the forehead; I fell down backward into the snow. As I was
trying to get to my feet again he struck me twice more; I
rolled over on my back and lay motionless.

Although combined with a sense of limitless downfall, the
feeling of joy which I subsequently experienced seems to me
an irrefutable proof that only physical suffering had the power
to allay the uneasy sense of shame due to the recollection of my
wrongdoing; that unlooked-for state which expressed itself in
a sort of childish gaiety and goodhumour, of cheerful willing-

ness, of complete detachment made me tremble and laugh at
the same time, and its intensity was such that I felt there were
no torments I could not have endured if I thought they would
hasten my rehabilitation by freeing me once and for all from
the weight of my remorse; for no ordeal was beyond my
strength, which seemed boundless. And this sort of ecstasy
explains why I plead not guilty to any charge of inertia, indolence, weakness, flaccidity and so on. From these to accusing me of cowardice, of course, there's only one step. And
yet, in order to shed light on some of my more puzzling attitudes, I have been obliged to dwell with often wearisome persistence on something I have always found hard to express,
at the risk of seeing a majority of my readers give up
the struggle, when everything inhibited me from inducing them
to share an emotion that was probably uncommunicable, of
doubtful interest to them and utterly lacking in the special
virtues belonging to ordinary emotions, but which, for the
understanding of the whole story and without regard to any
other consideration, I have been forced to emphasise.

He bent over me, swaying a little with an air of surprise; he
was panting hard, each breath ending with a stifled gasp as if
it were his last. A moment lapsed. I was out of breath myself
and gasping. My pulse throbbed painfully in my torn and
swollen lip. Perhaps the sight of my bruised face would dis-
hearten him from striking me again, perhaps he would think
it wiser to stop and turn on his heel, leaving me groaning and
bloodstained flat on my face in the frozen snow. I was afraid
he might have had enough of it; I hadn't yet, my punishment
seemed inadequate and so I tried to stand up again, hoping
to provoke him, by this unexpected recovery, to put me

definitely out of action. He resumed a defensive position. I
struggled to get up and realised that I could no longer feel
my legs. I knew that to keep up my role to the end I should
have to get up and pretend to strike him. Perhaps he would
kill me eventually, I did not want to die but if it had to be I
didn't mind. There was a moment's hesitation on both sides.
In spite of all the efforts I was making my attitude remained
tense and unconvincing. I saw that if I did not attack first he
would give up the game. I rushed at him, he had time to dodge,
his face dipped sideways in the moonlight. Then he lost
patience, leapt into the air and fell on me, feet foremost. He
struck out with all his might, my legs gave way and I dropped
on my knees. I heard him running off, then for a moment I
thought I heard the sound of bells ringing. I stayed there on
my knees, my head flung back, looking up at the black sky
with the tears pouring down my cheeks.

When I regained consciousness, I was lying on my side with
my right ear buried in the snow, my hands clutching the lapels
of my coat, hugging it closely round my chest. I felt a stabbing
pain in my forehead, between my eyes. I managed to twist
round on to my back and lay prostrate, motionless, staring
up into the fir-tree that rose above me, blank as a sleepwalker,
in the filmy white mist, while with one hand I clumsily felt
my face, which was numb with cold, and with the other I ex-
plored the layer of melting snow on which I was lying. I had a
distressing sense of being at the bottom of a crevasse from which
I should never be able to extract myself at the cost of the
wildest efforts, withdrawn forever from human eyes, lost to
the world, even if all the usual Sunday crowds should saunter
round me in serried ranks. I was painfully conscious of the

effect of the blows I had received; my splendid exaltation had
become boundless lassitude. The very memory of it makes me
shudder, less at the thought of my suffering than at the feeling
of my failure. Bitterly aware that the punishment I had sought
had not brought about the hoped-for change in me and
ashamed of having had recourse to so pitiful an expedient, I
felt nonetheless bound to submit to a fresh ordeal, which
would unquestionably be effective although at the cost of
sufferings even more atrocious and probably just as humiliating, a prospect so dreadful that I was filled with self-pity and
shed tears like a child : stupid tears, caused perhaps merely
by intense depression. And yet, apart from this apprehension,
being well aware that I could not remain unpunished, I felt
the urgent need to be cleansed of my sin and I longed ardently
to gain my own forgiveness, indeed this was the only spur that
could compel me to act amidst such deep distress. My misery
was intensified by the razor-sharp wind that whistled round
my ears, which were barely protected by a scanty muffler. The
cold might have been bearable had I been able to walk about
and restore the circulation to my frozen toes. But I should
have had to force myself on to my feet, and I did not feel
equal to such an effort. I managed to hoist myself up a little
and to lean against the trunk of the fallen tree. I stayed a long
while in this position, making no movement, with my legs
stretched straight in front of me, close together, like a statue
on some ancient tombstone, my hands resting on my knees, all
my attention concentrated on keeping my eyes open and staring up into the sky overhead, which was like a vault of wrought
iron. The lamps had gone out and day was beginning to break.
The lemon-yellow dawn flooded the empty garden, dripped

from branches and ledges, broke up the blocks of shadow
between the trees, and already smoke from the barges was drifting low over the opaque water. I felt cold and weary. I made
a feeble attempt to stand up, but without success; I soon had
to give up my efforts, panting hoarsely, and leaned stiffly against
the tree. My joints all seemed rusty and my limbs so much
dead matter. Why should I deny that there was something
contrived about this? With a little more tenacity I might have
managed without too much difficulty to rise to my feet; none
of my attempts had really been very painful, but amidst all
the anguish due to the bitter cold I felt a sort of temptation
to persist in my immobility; I succumbed to it as eagerly as, in
summer, I should have sprawled naked in the sun, although
now I got no actual pleasure from the tingling pain. At intervals I rubbed my frost-numbed ears to try and restore a little
life to them; but soon I found it quite impossible to endure
with patience what was beyond my strength, and I don't mean
only that cruel cold which saturated my whole skin and pierced
me to the marrow of my bones, but also the feeling of anguish
and desolation of which I only became really aware when I
caught myself moaning like a wounded animal, with a lack
of restraint encouraged by the surrounding silence. (A little
later I fostered this sadness, hoping thus to allay the fever
of my body; I set all sorts of bitter fancies running in my head,
brooding over my black loneliness, I wallowed deliberately in
the foul stream of my sin, I savoured its harsh bitter taste
complacently, the sense of guilt I thus harboured within me
served as an excellent refuge against physical suffering and I
told myself mechanically, without believing it, that I should
never again enjoy a ray of sunlight, a friendly smile, the sound

of a human voice; I chose to torture my brain and my heart rather than my timid flesh, and when I could not help granting myself a brief respite, not only was my face scalded with fiery tears but the thousands of needles seemed to pierce even the least vulnerable parts of my body in turn, with hallucinating regularity and precision.)

I felt, however, that by lying there prostrate and inactive I was yielding to some pernicious influence which sapped all my courage, and that I should never again be able to get up or go away. I made fresh efforts and succeeded in squatting on my heels, with my arms clasped round my knees, then I stood up for a moment, but my whole body reeled and spun round so that I lost my balance, stretched out both hands in front of me and was about to fall over on my face when I managed to steady myself by clutching at a branch. It seemed to me then that I had suddenly recovered all my strength, and to savour a foretaste of liberty I took a few steps, hesitantly at first and carefully keeping my right hand outstretched towards the tree trunk so that I could cling on to it in case I felt faint again, and then with growing confidence; but, afraid of overtaxing my strength, I halted and leaned against a tree; I stayed there a moment longer, pulled out my pocket mirror and ran a comb through my hair, picked up my hat, which, covered with snow on crown and brim, looked like an iced cake; I tried to brush it carefully with my hand and then with my hand-kerchief, and I straightened my coat, which was as crumpled as if it had been through the wash, scrubbed and wrung out. But just as I was about to brush down my trousers a sharp pain in the small of the back made me utter a cry; I toppled forward, and was only just able to protect my head with my hand. I fell, but promptly endeavoured to get up again, although I felt I had lost a great deal of my strength; I propped myself up on both arms to try and slide the rest of my body forward, thinking that if I could reach the dead tree it would serve to support me and, if I should once more feel that stabbing pain in the back, I would hold on to it until I was able to stand up properly. Contrary to my expectation, I managed this fairly easily; I was much less weak than I had fancied, and I succeeded in standing up with the help of a strong forked bough above my head. Once on my feet, unable to bring myself to take a single step, I stood for a few moments without moving, breathless, one hand clutching the bough, the other thrust deep into my pocket. And then an extraordinary thing happened.

Perhaps some day I may understand the reasons, which today elude me, for the curious sense of reassurance I felt even before I caught the sound of the childish voices. Could it be that, worn out by sleeplessness and the blows I had endured, I had dozed off for a brief moment, upright and open-eyed as horses do, and during my short sleep the sound of that cool, smooth-flowing song had acted on me as a soothing influence, whose effect lingered after my awakening, whereas I was still ignorant of its cause, which might perhaps explain my sudden start, followed by a sort of interruption of my anguish—as if threatening clouds had suddenly been rent apart to reveal a clear sky—to which was added the confident conviction that I could not enjoy everything without remorse, and a joy so intense that my physical pain—numbness, bruises on arms and legs, headache due partly to my last night's intoxication—was almost obliterated? The only certain thing is that there was an instant of quite unforeseeable ecstasy before the music reached my ears, or at least before I heard it clearly. (Although it does not obviously follow from the little I have said, I admit that my nerves may have been quicker than my senses to catch what they so urgently needed.) I could have sworn at first that these voices came from heaven or from the far end of the earth, whereas actually they were quite close by, borne aloft in the icy air in successive waves, voices as softly blurred and blended as a flutter of tumultuous wings. There was something so singular about them, so allusive and mysterious that I felt it could only be granted to a very small number of the elect to hear them; no doubt one had to be in a fitting state to receive them, and the flattering conviction took shape in my mind that since I enjoyed so rare a privilege, I must have been judged worthy of it, or better still, it was destined for me alone.

But this delightful illusion lasted only for an instant; reality, as I soon discovered, was of a far less thrilling nature; this music came to me not from heaven nor from the far end of the earth, but merely from over the top of that high wall bordering the canal, behind which, as I have already said, there rose, at certain times of day, the shouts and laughter of those sulky-faced children, priests in embryo, who could be seen trooping out on Thursdays with their mud-stained gowns sweeping the road, under the guidance of a smooth-chinned adult dressed exactly like themselves, who walked to and fro alongside of them, occasionally interrupting the monotonous buzz of talk with a curt and surly admonition.

My mistake gave me a clear insight into the crazy state of excitement I was in. It was wholly laughable, and yet the oddest part of it was that I did not feel inclined even to an ironic smile. Perhaps under normal circumstances I could have resisted the fascination of that music, which literally gripped me, and I should have wondered how such unattractive creatures were able to call forth from their inmost being a song so pure and so ineffable that it seemed miraculous, and since I was obliged to admit that they were the singers, how could they live unscathed behind those high walls which had been set between them and the lovely landscape over which my eyes lingered untiringly, and under the thumb of men like that great lout—but after all, how did I know that his surly looks did not conceal a store of precious qualities? Who trained and conducted that choir, in which each set of voices held its part with inflexible precision, if not one of the masters, and why not this one, who played the thankless part of sheepdog on their outings? In any case, all this ought to have puzzled and shocked me to the point of almost making me forget the marvellous sweetness of these voices, but in spite of myself, in spite of my determination never to be led astray by any random emotion (an attitude which is variously criticised among my acquaintances and has earned me the reputation, somewhat absurdly in my opinion, of being a calculating fellow) I was wholly subjugated by this music, which overwhelmed me, crushed me, annihilated me with its terrifying fullness—terrifying, because it left me so completely disarmed. (I have never needed the stimulus of suggestion to be moved by hearing my favourite works; they exercise over me a dominion from which I do not try to escape; I'm inclined therefore to think that through them alone can I reach the height of myself. On the other hand I am infinitely suspicious of the heady emotion

which, provided the setting and circumstances are favourable,
I get from hearing some quite trivial work, revoltingly senti-
mental or falsely pathetic, perfunctorily played by a third-rate
orchestra. Sitting alone in a café where three fiddles and a
tinkling piano perform a popular piece, or worse still, some
famous operatic aria which has pretensions to sublimity, if
I'm not careful I am liable to be overcome by a frenzy of
melancholy or delight of which I cannot honestly approve;
such emotion is too cheaply won, and so I have trained myself
to remain deaf to anything which, under pretence of exciting
my feelings, makes me absurdly maudlin; but unfortunately
I'm not calculating enough.)

Here, I made no attempt to exercise over my emotion a control which I foolishly reserved for feelings aroused by works
of whose worthlessness I was more or less clearly aware; in the
first place, this music was not vulgar, and secondly it stirred me
as no other could ever have done, I felt myself full of well-being
and overwhelmed by a serenity that was in all respects like
that I have described in connection with my first attack. I hope
I shall be forgiven if I abstain, for once, from trying to analyse
and define an emotion of which I was merely the bewildered
witness; it seems to me too individual, too personal and thus
too devoid of suggestive power to be worth dwelling on. What
can I say about it? Better in every respect to leave it on one
side, even though I cannot help giving it an important place
in my recollections, while reserving the right to mention, in due
course, one effect of it which was highly significant in that it
opened out surprising prospects to me, acting as a revelation,
like the sudden rending of a veil or the discovery of some
truth.

I shall confine myself this time to stating summarily, in a few lines, what struck me of the qualities peculiar to this music. As I listened to it in that public garden, my limbs numb with cold, it seemed to give out an intense, seductive warmth, due to the red glow of certain childish voices to which, however, there was added a sort of background curtain of gentler, utterly serene voices; for if, on the whole, there was about it something as soothing and enfolding as the atmosphere of an over heated room after a long wait in the cold air, it was above all through its dual character of freedom and joyful innocence that it moved me to the point of tears; but also by something strangely broad and clear like a sea breeze. In retrospect it seems to me that these voices also expressed utter indifference to human suffering, trampling underfoot all scruples, anxieties, doubts, all that forms the stuff of our cares, making mock of anguish with dazzling insolence (and yet never flinging at it the sort of morbid challenge that is so often absurdly forced and ostentatious). A pure and secret incantation, extraneous to the dull, heavy world we carry within ourselves, endowed with the magic peculiar to things that are free from the reek of sin, enchanting as the ideas called up by the words joy, spring, sunshine; issuing from a universe devoid of sexuality or blood, and yet unspoilt by the blemishes inherent in what is bloodless and sexless; its aerial grace contrasting with my dejected state, like that of a wounded beast; clear as a frosty night, refreshing as a bowl of spring water; ideal, in short, like whatever suggests the existence of a harmonious world, incommensurable with our copy of it, which can never be more than its wretched simulacrum. But what I must not fail to tell about this singing was my ineradicable conviction that it

F

brought me, like a familiar scent, some strange reminder of
a world as radically different from the scene of my present
distress as summer is from winter, so that amidst my joy I felt
a keen nostalgia, like that aroused in a man whose star is on
the wane by the recollection of his past glory, or that which
you feel if you heedlessly revisit the scene of a passion you had
thought yourself cured of. I still had to identify the episode in
my life with which it was connected, and I was the more
anxious to fix this precisely because, exclusively absorbed in
this importunate quest which prevented me from enjoying
the music, I felt myself becoming gradually obsessed by a
problem which I could never endure to leave unsolved; lacking any base from which to take my bearings, I was liable to
fret and worry and in the end to spoil all my pleasure. I wanted to clear up this point once and for all, and if need be I
should have stayed there till next morning, recalling my childhood, exploring it from top to bottom, examining its more
outstanding episodes in the hope of discovering there some sign
that would serve as a key and shed sudden light on the problem,
but should I have time to accomplish my task? Would the
music not suddenly vanish, and with it the thing that would
have enabled me to solve the riddle? And if so, why exhaust
myself to no end? In any case, it would no doubt be better not
to linger over such inquiries, which distracted my attention
from the very thing that had given rise to them and would
only result in withdrawing me from the beneficent sway of the
music, while I should have gained nothing which might justify
them. Actually my fears were unnecessary. For while I was
brooding over this, I gradually began to see daylight, I felt
convinced that I was on the right road, and had already

formed a rough idea of the atmosphere in which that incident had taken place which was to explain my nostalgia to me, although I could not yet define it nor locate it with any precision. Finally, as I wondered yet once more what could have given rise to this remembered sensation, the answer came to me like a flash of lightning. And now there gathered about those choirboys' voices memories belonging to various periods of my youth but roughly identical in content, all set in the chapel of that boarding school in Brittany where, overflowing with passionate eagerness, sharply resentful of the unjust restrictions I endured, I fostered all day long my pride and my hatred. And suddenly I remembered the triumphal way in which the afternoon sunlight fell in saffron-coloured shafts on the mosaic pavement, on the patterned lace of the altar cloth, gilding the five-branched candelabra held aloft by angels of flaking plaster, crowning with ephemeral haloes the heads of the smooth-cheeked, open-mouthed children; I remembered how the less pious among them used to bend forward, dropping their heads and cunningly holding their hands over their mouths when, tired of singing, they pretended to be absorbed in prayer, a sort of dissimulation at which I was past master, and which I practised frequently. And there recurred, too, to my mind the memory of one Sunday in May when I had noticed a big, full-feathered bird framed in one of the high windows, which were kept wide open to let out the sickening smell of incense : a grey bird clearly outlined against the shimmering young green of the chestnut tree which I saw every day resplendent in the sunlight like the glittering side of a ship—while I was wasting away, buried like a grub in my dark cold hole—and with what desperate, stubborn, senseless intentness I had striven to hear the song that came bubbling out of the bird's throat, thus challenging the torrential force of a Magnificat bawled out by two hundred voices, and how thrilling it was, when the music came to a solemn pause and a religious stillness settled below, to hear the bird up there warble its pure, shrill snatch of song with such ironic detachment that I grew dizzy with that absolute despair that is akin to happiness. But what I remembered above all was the state of unspeakable rapture I experienced during the Psalms; sometimes I joined in readily, mingling my unsteady voice with those of my companions, sometimes, if my hostile pride prompted defiance, I resisted with the full force of my will to autonomy, keeping my mouth tight shut except for a scornful pout, my head and shoulders held very straight, my eyes agleam with arrogance, hoping by the stiffness of my stance both to convey my disgust with these servile eulogies and to make public assertion of my liberty; and on such occasions, above all, I had a sense of suddenly becoming a tremendously impressive person—such as I still consider the man who, indifferent to the scandal he may create and defying unanimous disapproval, fights pluckily against huge odds to assert his views, even if these are misguided : the rebel who, refusing to conform to a state of things he disapproves of, although everyone else accepts it through weakness or self-interest, unhesitatingly braves the authorities who oppress him, fiercely determined not to yield until victory is won, however remote or illusory that may be; the prisoner at the bar, whether guilty or not, hounded by a society that's eaten up with respectability and common sense, in short all the oppressed on whom their lonely struggle confers an aureole of purity. To stand unmoving, obstinately deaf to that noble, solemn effusion which was nothing but a fraud, in a gestureless attitude of insubordination, to hold firm in face of the bleating prayers of all the rest, to be considered by my oppressors, by their lackeys and by Him who they professed to serve, as a black sheep or at least as an enemy whose very purity made him the more dangerous, to pose as a seductive rebel in the eyes of my schoolfellows, although I was bound to them by no complicity (save that which usually united us against our teachers), to inspire respectful fear in every heart—these were the wretched means —vulgar if they had not been a child's—by which I hoped to attain power, to cast off my chains, in a word to cheat myself for a brief while : the point was, after all, to make constraint bearable through the intoxication of proud self-confidence.

But, to revert to the choirboys' song, the nostalgia this aroused in me was not merely that mingled pleasure and regret which we always feel on reviving childhood memories which, seen in retrospect and with the bitter experience we have since gained, recur to us clad in such charming colours, but far more the disquiet I felt at the contradiction, now horribly evident, between what I had always expected to become and what I had in fact become : had I not dug with my own hands the unbridgeable gulf that separated me from my youth? Let me be clear : I was not lamenting the inability of an adult to escape from this harsh world, so hopelessly unfavourable to any mythical adventure, in which we struggle with spider-like ferocity, and then to gain entry by some vivid evocation of the past into that lost world on which men's eyes linger so sorrowfully—for my part I hold the world we call real the only one

worthy of our condition, and I have always preferred the
stark light of noonday to the mists of evening, the harshness of
truth to the subtleties of falsehood, nakedness to ornament.
On the contrary, what rent my heart was to discover in the
depths of my childhood something quite other than trivial
dreams : living passions, and for example my basic refusal to
compromise with what I loathed, my childish certainty that I
should some day have complete mastery over the world that
spread before me like an open field, my incapacity to accept
the fate allotted to me or to appease the feverish thirst of my
longings. My past reflected a strange image of myself, the mere
evocation of which cast a pitiless light on my present inadequacy; I felt I was discovering a conception of myself incompatible with what years of self-study had taught me. If I
suffered then, it was not so much through having to give up
the struggle for lack of enemies, as through feeling myself
hounded by enemies while prudence advised me not to engage
in open conflict with them for lack of weapons adequate to
defeat them, so that all I could do was to assume an attitude
of provocation and pure rage, or to taunt them with a perfectly
courteous laugh. But I would take comfort from the thought
that when at last the longed-for moment should come to take
the offensive, when I should at last be in a position to display
all my strength, flexibility and cunning, I should then enjoy
the rapture of victory. What was left me today of that firm
belief in myself, of that delight in destruction, of the more or less
open aggressiveness I directed against those who inflicted on
me a constraint I abhorred, the fascinated interest I took in
conquerors, gang leaders, insurgents, with whom, in my secret
heart, I felt a sense of intimate complicity, and of the naturally

rebellious frame of mind I showed in every sphere? As I had grown older my indifference had increased, nothing seemed to me worth any effort, and in consequence I no longer yearned, as I had once done, for revenge or conquest, but on the contrary for what would deliver me from these. Because today the noise of battle repels and wearies me, and I bear a mortal grudge against whoever rouses me forcibly from my indifference. To do nothing, to wait and see. . . .

This said, I must avoid implying that the nostalgia I have described was the essential element in the power of that music, which lay elsewhere and which would be inadequately defined if I merely stressed the uneasiness aroused by the evocation of what I had once held infinitely precious and necessary; I have insisted on this point, which is of secondary importance, because it seemed to provide the only key which would allow me to explore even a limited part of the contents of an emotion that would not fit into the framework of the real world. The predominant impression was, of course, an intense joy, such as wrings an ecstatic cry from a man about to embrace a woman he has long desired, or discovering at last, after many sleepless nights, some truth that puts him in touch with the secret essence of his being. And what was the meaning of that delicious heart's ease, that wild surge of my blood, if not that the triumphant joy ringing in my ears was intended to wipe out the grave misdeed I had committed the night before, from which all my suffering and self-disgust had sprung? I can find no other explanation for my sudden desire to take a few steps forward: now I felt certain that shame would no longer impel me to stumble involuntarily, to fall flat on the ground with my face buried in the snow or scarcely daring to look up at the

sky. For the first time that morning I had a feeling of physical
well-being, my limbs were glowing, I felt very strong, my joints
seemed supple and I resolved to test them without delay. As
I walked towards the canal I found to my delight that my legs
obeyed me perfectly and were eager to bear me wherever I
wanted.

But before going any further I wished to cast a final look
at the scene of my ordeal. In this twilight hour, while a few
large snowflakes floated singly to the ground in the clear icy
air, I felt it important to retain an exact impression of it. I
looked back therefore and saw the grotesque imprint left by
my numbed body on the muddy snow, stained with my own
blood. I forced myself to stand there a minute staring at that
place, that grey red-blotched sore surrounded by crimson
splashes, as hideous as an abscess on healthy flesh. Then I
turned away, to plunge eagerly into the stream of music which
was gradually swelling out in an ascending scale, infinitely
majestic. The voices seemed to be calling me with their echo-
ing responses and I could not, had I wished to, escape their
spell. It was for me that those voices were ringing out so urgently and with such wild solemnity, for me, for me alone,
there was no mistaking the fact, no evading the summons; they
were calling me! And yet I pretended to turn a deaf ear to
them and stood motionless, with my eyes fixed on the ground.
I told myself that I was still a free agent, that I might still
turn about and escape through the open gate which was less
than fifty yards away, that if I did not hurriedly leave this
garden I might perhaps have to give up all hope of doing so.
But I still stood obstinately there, looking round me without
moving my head : which was surely an admission that I had

understood, that I was indeed the object of that summons, that I was ready to obey. The incantation was growing so incredibly powerful that it took my breath away. And as it reached its climax, dizziness overwhelmed me, and some force seemed to sweep me forward. Conscious of my weakness, and moreover spellbound, I offered no resistance. As I drew nearer the canal I could see the water shining in the pale light of dawn and streaming on either side of the high wall that stood there as impenetrable, as meaningless, as anonymous as a boulder or a slab of rock. Now I could no longer be content with taking little careful steps, but ran helter-skelter across the snow. I clutched the railing as a starving man clutches food. And then it seemed to me that a thunderbolt was piercing my head behind my eyes, and the water glittering below me seared my eyelids and sent the blood rushing to my temples.

'Enough!' I sobbed aloud, 'enough!' After such singing, how could I ever dare open my mouth again?

III

And now I can see that you're burning to ask me a question. Go on! But, do first drop that ugly hostile attitude; are you still hoping to catch me out? Take care, I may be holding back an answer that will undermine the whole edifice of your irony. I'm willing to bet that you're shaking your head with a know-ing smile, as much as to say 'you can't fool me'; you probably think I'm resorting to intimidation for lack of any cleverer way out of my difficulty? In that case it's up to you to prove that you're not one of those impressionable people who let themselves be taken in by crude tricks. But first wait a minute,

please. Let me urge patience on the simple souls, if there are
any such among you, who have taken an interest in my story
and who, not wanting to be left unsatisfied, are gasping questions at me, their thoats dry and their eyes starting out of their
heads. . . . Well, it's quite true that I might have thrown myself into the canal, I hadn't thought of that, and it's also true
that I could have refrained from doing so. However, much as
I sympathise with those who are troubled by such legitimate
curiosity, and without wanting to offend anyone, truth obliges
me to declare that such a question would seem impertinent if it
were not so perfectly idiotic. Far be it from me, naturally, to
leave anything intentionally in suspense : it so happens that I
have the same answer ready for the most varied questions,
which simplifies everything and satisfies everybody. As for
those who won't waste their time wondering what I've been
getting at—for instance if I really took a header into that icy
water or if I turned away with a look of disgust—they would
probably like to know whether after listening to that sublime
music I did in fact never dare open my mouth again? I see.
What excites them is to learn *from my own lips* what they
already know! The painful sight of a man getting entangled
in his own contradictions as fast as he tries to unwind
them! They're hoping for a laugh, I shall not give them that
pleasure. They may think they're fooling me, but I shall fool
them.

Imagine a conjuror who, tired of imposing on the credulity
of the crowd whom he has hoaxed with his illusions, takes into
his head one fine day to exchange the pleasure of enchanting
them for that of disenchanting them, thus reversing the usual
trend of vanity and risking the loss of all the advantage gained

from his reputation as a miracle-worker. Make no mistake about it, it's from no belated but laudable desire for honesty that he chooses to disclose his secrets one by one with the deliberate meticulousness of a watchmaker taking a clock to pieces, he has no scruples of that sort, he's moved merely by a delight in destroying what he has created and blighting the enthusiasm he has aroused, and so he lays all his cards on the table, making his subtlest tricks seem commonplace, relishing the disappointment of those whom he had astounded, coming down of his own free will from the pinnacle on which his dupes had set him, eagerly watching for the first flicker of disillusionment in their eyes, which only yesterday were wide with childish wonder, and should he see the slightest gleam of faith still lingering on those saddened, feebly smiling faces, he promptly extinguishes it with the same zeal with which he had previously fostered it. Am I that cruel man, that lunatic?

In any case I make no pretence of being a victim, I am ready to admit the justice of most of the charges brought against me, and if there is one accusation to which I confess I've laid myself open, it is that of speaking inconsiderately; it's quite true that I have been holding forth unceasingly without rhyme or reason, introducing irrelevant details which interest nobody but myself, it is true that I have often tried, by some play-acting instinct, to pose as something that I'm not, to attribute to myself feelings which I have never had the occasion to experience or actions I was incapable of accomplishing, in order to give piquancy to a life which was devoid of it; it is true, too, that I had the effrontery to deny what I held most dear and to praise what I have always professed to hate. You have undoubtedly every right to blame me for talking in a high-

minded tone about sincerity when my principal concern was
to twist truth to make it more exciting or more plausible; not
to mention my roulades, my contortions, my subterfuges, my
grimaces. Granted, I'm a *bavard,* a chatterer, a harmless and
boring chatterer, just as you are yourselves, and a liar into the
bargain like all chatterers, that's to say like all men. But how
does that give you the right to reproach me bitterly for a vice
which is your own? I can't be expected to stop in my corner,
silent and modest, listening to high-sounding words from
people whom I won't admit to be more experienced or more
thoughtful than myself. Who's going to cast the first stone at
me?

What you seem least of all disposed to forgive me for is my
uneasy conscience. When one is ashamed of being a chatterer,
you say, one's only got to hold one's tongue. Agreed. But does
this deplorable impulse which we have in common constitute
a defect for which those who are not ashamed of it have the
right to criticise me? I'm afraid I consider that my conscience,
even if it is uneasy, is better than your blindness. Is it really
true that, enraptured by the beauty of that music, I uttered
a vow that bound me henceforward to maintain a decent silence? Am I then a horrid perjurer? And should you per-
tinently remind me of the shame I experienced after my major
attack, only to pretend subsequently to be surprised that it did
not cure me of my vice, I shall tell you . . . what shall I tell
you, actually? I shall find it only too easy to ruin your cheap
effects. It's not my fault if your quibbling makes me smile. It
remains to be seen whether I really heard that music, whether
I really experienced that shame. I shall tell you then that the
fact that I have taken the trouble to give an exact description

of each of them doesn't mean that their authenticity can never again be disputed by anyone, by myself to begin with. Isn't it possible that my imagination may work a little faster than my memory? You may think I'm going rather far : to pretend to doubt one's own statements is the height either of impertinence or of dishonesty. And suppose I were not pretending to doubt, and suppose I were not in doubt, and suppose I knew quite well what to believe about the truth of my remarks and suppose, in fact, all my chatter consisted of lies? You flounce away angrily : 'Then to hell with you!' I cannot urge you too strongly to consider the situation calmly, don't feel you've been wasting your time listening to lies, since you have had the privilege of witnessing an attack of talkativeness, which was surely more instructive than reading an account of it, even one innocent of any literary intention. Be kind enough not to resent my having imposed on your credulity by insinuating, without your knowledge, a few truths in the midst of so many lies which I have passed off to you as truths, in the belief, which has been confirmed, that the former would be indistinguishable from the latter. I am quite ready to make due apology to those whom I have hoaxed, I can assure them that I don't in the least care about having the last word, I merely ask to be allowed to explain my case quietly, since it's probably no worse than some of yours, I think we shall come to some agreement provided you allow me time to go back and start again at the beginning in order to clear up, once and for all, a misunderstanding which has gone on too long, and to show that it was not based on anything so serious as we may have believed.

Who has not felt, at least once in his life, a longing to raise

his voice, not with the quite reasonable hope of charming his
hearers nor with any pretensions to instructing them, but more
simply to satisfy his own caprice? And even so, as I said at the
beginning, he must be firmly convinced that somewhere or
other there are ears willing to hear him—and as I shall show
later, he must use a great deal of cunning to secure his hearers'
sympathy by making them want to hear what he's going to
say: a speaker finds it curiously encouraging to have a human
face in front of him. It doesn't really matter if you haven't a
great deal to say, indeed you may quite well have nothing at
all to say; I don't see why anybody need protest when I declare
that speaking and expressing oneself are two different things.
Is there anyone dishonest enough to claim that he never opens
his mouth except to communicate an idea or to let people hear
the charming sound of his voice? He's a humbug! When you
open your lips you may not know, perhaps, what you're going
to say, but the conviction that you'll find the flow of words
you need, under the circumstances and in the excitement these
arouse in you, emboldens you to launch out at random: the
important thing is to satisfy your urge to talk without delay; it
usually happens that the words come promptly in answer to
your appeal. However, it may equally happen, and here we
touch on my own personal case, that words remain refractory,
and then you experience an anguish akin to that of a paralysed
man trying to escape from imminent danger. Some people, I
know, find it hard to resign themselves to the impossibility of
satisfying their need, others stay on their guard, depending
more or less sincerely on chance to deliver them, waiting
quite passively for their affliction to be cured, gradually growing used to it, unless they seek to pass it off as strength of mind,

in which case they pretend to despise a desire which their impotence forbids them to satisfy.

When I'm eager to talk, I never think of forcing myself to keep silence, and yet the last thing I want to do, and I say this without affectation, is to pour out my soul in public or even into one friendly ear. Nothing is further from me than the care some men take to expose their self-knowledge to the general gaze. And yet it is useless to hope to open your lips if you cannot conquer your profound aversion to the glare of the footlights. You are condemned to appear on the stage, you must resign yourself to playing the mountebank there. For my own part I make no claim to modesty : it's all one to me whether I show off or remain in obscurity, but no scruple will deter me from laying traps for my listeners' trustfulness if I think the interest aroused by my lies can help me to satisfy my vice.

No, my preoccupation is of a lower order. Isn't my imagination liable to fail me, in the first place? Where shall I find something to chatter about? For it's obvious to everyone that I cannot merely open my mouth to produce inarticulate sounds or a string of random words : I've already said, and I shall not reiterate, that a talker never talks to empty space, he needs to be stimulated by the conviction that someone is listening to him, even if mechanically; he does not require any repartee, indeed he barely seeks to establish any live connection between his listener and himself; although it's true that his loquacity rises to a pitch of wild exaltation under the spur of agreement or contradiction, it can sustain itself quite well in face of indifference or boredom.

I was thus in the throes of anguish at the impossibility of

taking the first step; in vain did I collect my thoughts, close
my eyes—like a preacher about to embark on a long sermon
—hoping that silence would provide the inspiration and give
me the time necessary to concoct some memory that would
be plausible and prolific of developments, all these efforts only
served to confirm my belief that my imagination was cold and
dried up. However, my desire grew more vehement, and my
ambition to compete with those whose eloquence I envied
made my throat ache; I did not want impotence, any more
than pride, to frustrate my frantic wish to indulge in this activity. And then I suddenly realised, in a flash, that what I
was seeking far and wide lay close at hand. I would talk about
my urge to talk.

But how could I have performed this task lightheartedly?
It has never been held very pleasant to open one's heart to
unfriendly folk who are resolutely inclined to see the worst in
everything about them, and the admission of a vice that nobody dares secretly recognise as his own could only call forth
ironic comments from the more hypocritical listeners and a
chorus of unbridled abuse from the more spiteful of them.
Wasn't it mad to risk one's reputation, to expose oneself to
sarcasm for the mere pleasure of talking? Moreover it lay
entirely in my power to confuse the trails I had so carefully
laid. What prevented me from touching up a truth whose ex-
plosive qualities I dreaded? Why should I be so scrupulous
about drawing a faithful likeness of myself, which could only
deserve contempt, when I could arouse pity by cunningly in-
voking illness as an excuse for irresponsibility? My chief concern, then, was in the first place to give to an entirely invented
story such an appearance of exactness and logic that it might

seem to my interlocutor that, scrupulously obeying the reliable data provided by memory, I had never yielded to the temptations of imagination nor allowed any play to the works in my narrative; in the second place, to give plausible life to certain purely fictitious figures (including that which I passed off as my own) whom I introduced as actors or walkers-on in a drama which was in fact entirely made up for the furtherance of my purpose, while taking care to leave about them no suspicious vagueness which might cast doubt on their authenticity or my own sincerity. The better to convince the more demanding of my readers, I pretended to renounce those effects which serve to show off the author's skill rather than to cling more closely to the truth, and those fine bursts of eloquence which are usually typical of counsels' speeches and of sermons, together with certain tricks of my own which, on other occasions, I have used to great advantage. It will be remembered that with an ostentatiousness which might just as well have passed for excessive modesty I did not fail to emphasise the deliberate bareness of my style, with hypocritical regrets that a certain monotony was the inevitable price paid for honesty. But this pretence of foregoing artifice was itself an artifice, and a far more devious one. If I happened to tell a lie, it was only so as to allow me subsequently to make humble confession of it; true, I had a deplorable tendency to use evasions, to talk nonsense in order to conceal or postpone what I dared not tell, but, smitten with remorse, I immediately corrected myself, which proved that I was not acting with evil intent, and you could obviously trust a man who was so anxious not to fall into the common vice of disguising truth. (Allow me to express my surprise, by the way, that none of you has ever troubled to lift the veil with which, out of modesty or cowardice, I have concealed myself. Do you even know who is speaking to you? And yet you feel more sympathy and respect for a man who introduces himself modestly by his own name, there is in fact a certain nobility about offering oneself up to criticism as a willing victim. Am I a man, a shadow, or nothing, absolutely nothing? Have I gained any substance through chattering to you all this while? Do you picture me as possessing other organs besides my tongue? Can I be identified with the owner of the right hand that is setting down these words? How are you going to find out? Don't expect him to denounce himself of his own accord. Who, in his place, would not rather remain anonymous? I am sure he would protest with sincere indignation if I undertook to hand him over as a prey to the wrath of some and the contempt of others. Does he know himself what I am made of, assuming that I am made of something? He has every intention of keeping aloof from this discussion, he washes his hands of my errors. You can shout your loudest: 'Author, author!' I wager he'll not show the tip of his nose; we all know what cowards such people are. Now, I ask you: what good is a label to you if the goods are of dubious quality? Suppose you should eventually know the name, age, title and profession of the man who has never stopped lying to you about himself, would you be any better off? He has said nothing true about himself, you'd better conclude that he doesn't exist.)

I am not vain enough to believe that I have succeeded in winning your support, either by the self-confident tone I had tried to maintain until just recently nor by the logical connection I have somewhat laboriously woven through the epi-

sodes of an adventure which is rather too obviously incredible,
and for instance, if I had not got you to swallow my dissertations on the pathological character of my vice I should be fully
satisfied; has anyone been able to listen without laughing to
my account of what I pompously described as my attack? I
need hardly tell you that I have never experienced attacks of
that sort. They merely served to conceal the shame that I feel
at being afflicted with the inglorious vice in which, much as I
dislike the thought, we all indulge with the same frenzy. Now,
don't go and imagine that I have lied so brazenly for the crude
pleasure of seeing you taken in by my most fantastic tales; I
have not consented without long deliberation, of which this
confession is the proof, to lay snares for your trustfulness; my
sole preoccupation, which should suffice to clear me of any
charge of duplicity, was to arouse your interest and maintain
it by having recourse to certain misleading effects, whose only
aim was to lead you more surely where I wanted to lead you,
namely to the present point. But I hope you're going to ask me
why I have busied myself with such strange zeal about ex-
posing my own frauds and, should you have no intention of
asking me such a question, I have some reason to think that
you will ask it when I shall no longer be there to answer. So
I'm answering it right away, which will at least have the effect
of clearing me from the unjust suspicion of evading anything
that embarrasses me, while giving me an opportunity to satisfy
what is left of my urge to chatter. I might reply that belated
remorse has induced me to reveal what I had taken such care
to conceal, that my native horror of falsehood has finally con-
quered my shame, that it has suddenly appeared to me wrong
to persist any longer in deluding those of my readers who had

been courteous enough to follow me up till now; I might also
reply, ascribing somewhat less lofty feelings to myself, that I
took a sort of perverse delight in undeceiving my own dupes,
that I like exhibiting my own defects or that I enjoyed being
spurned by those I had led on with false charms, or else I might
mention the childish pleasure we often take in destroying what
we have built with our own hands at the cost of unremitting
labour. But of course I should still be telling lies. The truth is
that, feeling my imagination fail and yet reluctant to hold my
tongue, I could think of nothing better than to disclose my
swindle to those who were its victims, and you have seen that
I haven't spared you a single detail. I flung myself so eagerly
on to this fresh topic only because I had nothing else available
at the time to feed my foolish and unfortunate passion. I had
substituted the ludicrous for the pathetic. But I was holding
my own, and that was the main thing : I was talking, I was
talking, what bliss! And I'm still talking now.

I meet with severe criticism. I am disliked, and I know that
by probing the reasons for your dislike I can only make you
dislike me more, but it's not merely insolence, nor tactlessness,
nor lack of modesty, nor an affectation of sincerity or perspicacity—although there is certainly something of all these—
that discredits me in your eyes. Why have I exposed myself
when I could have kept safely in the background? Why have
I drawn attention to myself? Why am I now inscribed on
the enemy's short list? I have sacrificed the delights of obscurity to my vice, and by a cunning fraud I have tried to put
you on a false scent, seeking to cover up my own emptiness
and at the same time to justify my inconsistencies—it was a
clever way of distracting attention and shuffling the cards—

and, for instance, when to end up with I admit that I have positively nothing to say, you can catch something like a note of pride in my voice. And even now I am reviving your antagonism by trying to see clearly into myself : anyone who examines his own imperfections with some concern for objectivity you consider ostentatious; you think I obviously pride myself on my gift of penetration, and that is odious too. So that if I had any imagination I should be reduced to talking about any other subject rather than myself. Now I think I can clearly see the unflattering picture people may form of me, and hear the unkind remarks you are going to make about me, and the more I accumulate specious arguments for my defence, the more hateful and contemptible I appear in your eyes. But I care little whether you are irritated by my constant concern with describing myself in every detail, whatever I may say, which will never express more than my pretensions, will always serve to prove me in the wrong, whether I examine my case in all seriousness or adopt a humorous tone. Whatever I say, even if my remarks are wholly inoffensive, I shall speak in such a way that you will always blame me. You think I'm an impostor, a presumptuous, provocative, good-for-nothing fellow, and so forth. An idler indulging in facile self-expression, you can't bear to hear any more of my stories, you loathe every word that comes out of my mouth, it's more than you can stand ! And yet, as I've already said, I find no pleasure in making myself an object of disgust to you, in grovelling in the dirt at your feet; I've gone in for a very different sort of enjoyment, which may be just as morbid, that can't be helped—I mean the pleasure of talking, and you see I'm still talking and talking away.

But just as there comes a moment when the liveliest flame begins to writhe and dip smokily, flickers and finally goes out, so even the most inveterate chatterer eventually feels a growing soreness at the back of his throat, his eyes grow hazy from staring too long into those of his listener, in which they were straining to revive a gleam of interest, he's no longer very sure what he wanted to say nor how to say it, and he longs for some welcome respite, so that something happens to him which he could not have foreseen and which the other fellow had ceased to hope for. Silence—that silence for which he feels that mingled terror and longing aroused by the mere imminence of something which is both desirable and dangerous, wonderful and dreadful, that silence to whose arid laws he had never consented to bow, which he has never ceased to hate, but to which nonetheless he remains bound by an aching nostalgia, he catches himself summoning it with secret wishes, even though a lingering vestige of pride and awe still restrains him from taking the first step (and it is with joyful relief that his victim notices those signs of fatigue which are also signs of his own release). But knowing his weaknesses, how could he hope to be happy for long in a drab and sterile region which he dislikes? He finds himself rather in the state of a man who, thinking he has done everything possible to avert disaster, has to yield to the evidence that the game is lost, utterly lost; under the circumstances of its ending he is deprived even of the pride of having played it.

I shall be silent, then. I'm going to be silent because I am worn out by my excesses: words, words, so many lifeless words which seem to have lost the very meaning of their faded sound. I wonder if there is anyone there still listening to me? For some while now I've been conscious of stubbornly keeping up a ridiculous and futile monologue in a public square from which the audience have all gone away in disappointment, shrugging their shoulders, but I am so puerile that I delight in the thought that my revenge will consist in leaving them for ever in ignorance of whether I was still lying when I pretended to lie. What else can I say? I am not equal to my vice, nor have I ever claimed to be. But on the whole I have succeeded in my object. I have gained some relief, and nobody shall tell me it was not worth while. And now I'm weary. Come on, gentlemen, I've told you I'm not keeping you any longer!

THE CHILDREN'S ROOM

THE CHILDREN'S ROOM

No WORDS can convey the bewilderment and shame he feels at standing there eavesdropping behind the half-open door of the children's room. He is aware that it would be more sensible to go back to his own room, but he is astonished by his inability to retrace deliberately the few steps he has just taken absent-mindedly, if not in a daze; he is astonished, above all, by that uneasiness which is surely disproportionate to its cause, for after all, if he has never hitherto made his way to the children's room nor, probably, any of the children to his, what moral scruple, what domestic convention forbids him to do so? And now that he finds himself as though by accident behind this door, he is astonished that this indefinable disquiet, unrelated to any sense of having broken a law, betrayed a secret or taken part in any questionable activity, far from driving him from his post keeps him rivetted to it; he knows that nothing can persuade him to leave his post, he knows therefore that he will not leave it, subtly justifying his decision by the need to understand through experience why he ought to have done so and why he has been unable to.

He knows too—for it seems to him that he knows everything—that this argument is specious. In fact, he feels that he knows everything and can do nothing, and it is from his clear-sightedness and his impotence that he derives the keenest pleasure as well as a quite groundless sense of guilt. In support of his decision he might justifiably plead irresponsibility as well as non-premeditation. He had not had to argue with himself, even summarily, whether or not to listen at the door; he was unexpectedly struck by the sound of childish voices, and by then it was already too late for him to escape, just as a sin is consummated at the first covetous glance. But even if this other argument had been sufficient to convince him of the inanity of his scruples, it would not have dispelled them, or if it had, he might as well promptly give up his watch outside the children's room, since it is precisely in order to seek enlightenment as to the nature of these scruples that he is taking such an exaggerated interest in the chatter of these idle schoolboys.

'Not now, no! Let's keep still.'

Insignificant and yet of capital importance, the first sentence that strikes his ear arouses in him a mysterious curiosity and stays him from returning to his own room.

'Keep still, oh I say! Are we going to talk then?'

'You're not obliged to, in fact we shall be grateful if you don't. Follow George's example!'

He recognises the voice of his nephew Paul, but who may this George be?

'Let's have some fun getting George to talk, shall we?'

'Good idea! Come on, George, why have you gone dumb?'

'He's not dumb, he refuses to speak.'

'Well then, George, why do you refuse to speak?'

'He won't speak. He only speaks in school. I tell you he won't answer.'

'I'd be curious to hear George's voice now that he doesn't use it any more.'

'Paul could tell us what it's like, he's in George's form.'

'You know people always put on the same voice to say their lessons.'

'Paul's right. Saying lessons isn't talking. Why won't you talk, George, answer us!'

'George, we're speaking to you, answer!'

'I tell you he won't answer.'

'If we were to torture him, wouldn't he end up by talking?'

'By crying, you mean! But then you might as well tickle him to make him laugh. Let's leave him alone.'

'Anyone would think that he was here to go through a test, and that we were here to put him through it.'

'Not at all. He looks quite at ease, doesn't he?'

'More so than we do. We've offended him, but it's we who are offended by his silence.'

'Is it because we've offended him that he's sulking?'

'How can we know, Jeannette, since he hasn't told us?'

Jeannette? But he doesn't recognise her voice, while Paul's voice seems to be answering remarks made by Paul in some-one else's. Can Paul be acting the parts of imaginary inter-locutors in turn, and if so, why is he playing others' parts in his own voice and his own part in another's voice? Or if, on the contrary, there are several children in the room, can this un-known George whose silence they are discussing be the only fictitious character, whom they have deprived of speech for the sake of the game while cunningly pretending to urge him to talk, as if his silence were the result of a whim and not a neces-sary result of the *mise en scène*? But of all the children inside the room, this George is the one whose presence seems to him least in doubt, for George benefits from the prestige of his silence whereas the rest, borrowing one another's voices, seem

to merge into a single person, always changing, always inde-
terminate. That is what makes less plausible the hypothesis of
a twofold impersonation.

'How can we know, Jeannette, since he hasn't told us?'

'I can see by his face that he's offended.'

'What an imagination! I can see no expression at all on his
face, except an ironic one. He's laughing at us, and we're
fools to have given him cause. George, we'll allow you to hold
your tongue.'

'George, we implore you to hold your tongue! But wouldn't
it be wiser to order him to turn his face to the wall?'

'Why not block his ears? No, I'm against that! It would
be like banishing him from the room, where he's never refused
to come and play with us.'

'But Paul, surely this time he could neither refuse nor accept!'

'He's come, so I assume he's accepted.'

'And he was quite right to come, for if he'd refused he'd
have broken his vow. He's come as he always used to come,
every Thursday; his presence, to which we're accustomed,
isn't as remarkable as his absence would have been.'

'Which doesn't prevent us from holding forth about his
presence! But I think we're being very solemn this evening,
and I'm getting bored.'

'What about you, George, are you bored?'

'It's not time to ask him that yet. I was just about to discuss
a very boring subject. But boring chiefly for George, who's as
familiar with it as I am. I mean the school rules. Now listen.'

'No, Paul, we've not come here to listen to you talking about
your school!'

'Wasn't it you who suggested getting George to speak?'

'I don't see the connection. Nor, obviously, does Tony. And you, George, do you see the connection?'

'Stop teasing George! Do you expect him to answer you?'

'Yes, I think we can depend on his saying something inadvertently.'

'If you managed to make him speak inadvertently we'd have no reason to congratulate you, for he wouldn't really have spoken at all, and afterwards he'd only be the more careful, besides which he'd never forgive us for catching him out with a trick. We must keep the rules of the game, Jeannette.'

'What rules? And what game are you talking about?'

'Paul, Paul! I think the time has come for you to tell us about your school rules. This young lady and myself are anxious for instruction, albeit tedious.'

'Albeit, albeit!' and all the children, except the last, speaker and presumably this George, make fun of the boy or girl who, in Paul's pedantic voice, had expressed the desire for instruction from Paul; and then they all burst out laughing. On this chorus of laughter there follows a silence so prolonged that he wonders for a moment whether the children haven't disappeared without his knowledge into the reception room next door, but that room, he knows, can be reached only through the passage where he is standing watch. Straining his ears, he seems to hear a busy mouse-like scurrying behind the door, as though furniture were being carefully moved about, with brief intermittent whispered orders: 'Here. No, there! Quick, give it me!' and so on. Any remarks they make, any steps they take are cautiously controlled, like those of scene-shifters between two tableaux, behind a makeshift curtain. Then Paul's voice rings out through the room, so firm, so severe, so full of com-

punction that only its high pitch betrays the fact that it is not
an adult's. Each word is carefully articulated, as by one who
means to be obeyed and whose commands will not be repeated.
It is the speech of authority in the mouth of a child. Amplified
by its majestic tone, Paul's voice seems to come from a great
height, as though from a mountain or a balcony, and in fact
it is quite possible that he has clambered up for the occasion,
the better to dominate his audience, on to a scaffolding of
furniture, hastily piled up on his orders by the other children.

'Of course I am not going to speak to you about the school
rules as originally drawn up by the founder in some eighty-
odd articles, for nobody could listen to those with a straight
face except our teachers, and neither George, so far as I know,
nor I myself have learned that venerable text by heart; the
spirit of it has vanished into thin air and even the most capti-
ous of our masters only refers to it as a last resort, in order to
catch us out, and then, as I've noticed, most reluctantly! I tell
you, there are no other rules than those which each of us, even
the most rebellious, brings with him when he first goes to
school; that is why we cannot escape them, however much we
argue to the contrary and however loudly we proclaim our
disgust with such restrictions, thereby justifying the arrogance
of our masters who, unwarrantably, claim to be the authors
of these rules and who regretfully carry them out. It is thus
more painful to comform to them, and more impossible to
avoid doing so, than to any rule imposed by our masters. Let
us assume, to begin with, that any breach of the rules makes
the culprit liable to. . . .'

'But Paul, that means you're siding with the masters!'

'And yet we must make ourselves liable to punishment, since

by keeping the rules we render them invalid, and without rules. . . .'

'Where would be the pleasure of disobedience? Bravo, Paul! You've succeeded in making George smile!'

'George is smiling at your ignorance! Let me tell you, foolish brat, that there is no pleasure in breaking rules, but on the contrary there's a very considerable pleasure in hearing oneself sentenced to punishment.'

'Well, I don't like punishments at all, whether I've deserved them or not.'

'You don't like punishments, but it's a fact that you like having them inflicted on you, whether you deserve them or not.'

'That's not true!'

'Let's assume Paul's right and let's see what he's trying to prove.'

'That. . . . Now you've disturbed my train of thought! George, please come to my help, since you've been following my argument without interrupting me!'

'As if George would be taken in by such a clumsy trick! No, Paul my boy, you've not succeeded in allaying his suspicions! We'd just been blaming you for siding with the masters. . . .'

'And I think I replied that by incurring punishment we strengthened the rules we ourselves had created and thus made our masters our servants.'

'These rules may be your own creation, but those who impose them on you are certainly your masters! So what's the good of your hair-splitting? And for a start, what are these famous rules?'

'As you're still too young to learn them for yourself at school, George and I will try to give you some idea of them.'

'George indeed? I'd like to hear that!'

'George is speaking with my voice.'

'What cheek! Or is that another trick to get George to protest? And you who accused Jeannette of not playing fair!'

'Stop quarrelling! Well, Paul, what about those rules?'

'I'm coming to them.'

He wonders if it is to give greater solemnity to his declaration that Paul allows himself a long pause? Or is he standing rigid, open-mouthed, like an actor who has forgotten the first word of his speech? Or has he perhaps given up any attempt to keep a straight face, and joined in the sudden merriment of his companions, whose smothered laughter is sounding behind the door? And what if the children, having tacitly agreed to improvise on the first topic that occurred to them in order to baffle the unwanted witness whose presence they suspected behind the door, have now found their inspiration flagging, or feel unable to carry on a conversation on so grave and grown-up a tone without bursting into laughter? What if his persistent disquiet results from an obscure sense of being hoaxed by a gang of mischievous youngsters? But just as he is considering leaving his post to avoid the shame of being caught in the act of spying, Paul's voice rings out again through the room, grave, persuasive, sententious as ever, dispelling his fears, arousing his curiosity.

'Once you have passed inside the doors of the school you are bound by a discipline whose rules are inscribed nowhere but in yourself. Should you seek to break free of them, you would always be aware of your wrongdoing, even though your masters should condone or ignore it. It can thus be said that from that moment you are bound by self-imposed obligations, which proves that the rules laid down by the masters are super-fluous, nonsensical, inapplicable.

'Now to come to our own set of rules. They cannot be defined and so, unlike those of the teachers, they cannot be learned. Once you've passed inside the doors of the school they cling to you like a uniform identifying you with those inside and distinguishing you from those outside. To discard this would be like passing out through the door again.'

'But can you explain to us how the rules took possession of you when you passed inside the school doors?'

'Outside the school precincts the rules no longer haunt us. They are as vague as memories, however hard we try to call them to mind. But to satisfy your curiosity allow me to enact, with George, a few of the scenes which may help us in our attempted reconstruction. Let's imagine, then, that this room is the place in which the rules hold sway. George shall be the master.'

'And we're your schoolfellows. . . .'

'You may be my schoolfellows, at a pinch, but, you silly kids, you can't take me for a schoolfellow of yours. . . . The scene we're going to play can only be imagined and lived through by George and myself : you are merely the spectators, or at most the "extras".

'I have said that this room was to be the place where the rules hold sway, and now we shall give the name Jim to the boy who's going to enter it for the first time, through this door. You've got to go out of the room under your own name and then to come in under the name of Jim, as though into a place from which Jim has never gone out before, since presumably he has never before gone into it.'

'Unless he's been home for the holidays. . . .'

'Of course, but then he would only recognise this room as being the place where the rules hold sway, and certainly not the place where we meet every week. Let's begin at once. Now we're going to see Jim come in through this door !'

At these words, spoken in Paul's voice, the door in front of him opens and he has just time enough to fling himself against the nearest wall, thus avoiding the sight of the children assembled in the room, but not that of the child who has just come out of it. He is surprised and at first relieved not to recognise his nephew in this schoolboy in shorts, who stares at him unseeing, as if he were alone in the passage or were deliberately refusing to take any notice of his manœuvre. But his confusion is increased by the fact that although the features of this childish face seem familiar, its expression is, on the contrary, so strange to him that he feels convinced he has never seen it before. The silent confrontation lasts only for the time it takes the boy to close the door and open it again, but it is long enough to disturb him deeply; he is shaking from head to foot, his eyes fixed on those of the young creature, whose lack of curiosity might have offended him had it not arisen, he feels sure, from some mysterious blindness (for surely had the child seen him or suspected a grown-up of spying in the darkness of the passage, he could not have controlled his vexation or embarrassment, no matter how he tried to disguise them under a pose of bravado or nonchalance. Now the gaze that looks straight through him is innocent of any effrontery, and reflects only his own absence; in the suspended gesture of the hand grasping the door knob, in the expectant, almost defiant forward movement of the whole body from shoulder to knee, there is nothing constrained or studied, he sees there only the awkwardness of extreme youth).

'Come in!' orders Paul's voice behind the door. Just as he is about to take advantage of this opportunity to peer forward, trying to see a corner of the scene, the door is slammed in his face and he springs back, infuriated with his failure, mortified and almost incapable, this time, of resigning himself to the role of an invisible listener. His disappointment is so keen that he considers forcing his way into the room, but he gives up this idea for fear that his intrusion might not pass as unnoticed as his presence in the passage has apparently been by the boy who has just left it.

'Now it's Jim who is coming in through this door,' Paul's voice announces. 'And it's Jim who must answer the questions we shall put to him, in order to help him and bring his inner conflict to light. Jim, where are you?'

'In the playground,' comes the reply in what seems still to be Paul's voice, except that it is now weak, faltering, as though in distress.

'What are you afraid of?'

'Such chaos! Such shouting!'

'Answer my question!' Paul's voice orders severely.

'I'm afraid of seeming different from the rest because of my ignorance of the rules,' says Paul's voice, once again as scared as a lost child's.

'Your ignorance? On the contrary, the fact is that you're too much of a novice to stop thinking about them. Aren't you letting yourself be paralysed by the fear of not conforming to rule?'

'It's true, I should like to be one of those whom experience has made carefree and independent. If only I could play as

they do, I should not have to endure their disapproval and
their mockery!'

'Let time pass and you'll be able to play as whole-heartedly
as they do!' And Paul's voice explains in an aside: 'That's how
Jim becomes obsessed by the rules, through over-conscientious-
ness; he feels crushed by the extent of his new duties, he is
alarmed by their strictness, how can he think himself equal
to fulfilling them, how can he help feeling perpetually at fault,
exhausted as he is by enumerating all those regulations and
terrified by the thought that he may infringe them through
ignorance, whereas once inside the school doors he knows them
as well as his schoolfellows and better than his masters, whose
reprimand he will endure only in order to test their zeal and
their servitude. And now we should let a few days go by.
Where have you got to now, Jim?'

'But how can I explain, how can I explain to you who have
never passed through those doors, how can I describe in the
present tense what can only be described in the past—I mean
for instance the dank smell of paper and ink, and the smell
of other people's toothpaste and of the chlorine disinfectant
in the lavatory, the ebbing tide of shouts in the playground,
punctuated by the irregular clanging of the bell that announces the end of break, and the loud slamming of desks,
you who know nothing of all this, how can I hope to make you
understand what I'm describing thus only because I'm re-
creating in front of you what I heard and felt this morning,
and not, of course, what I'm experiencing while talking to
you now.'

'But it was to Jim I spoke!' exclaims Paul's angry voice.
'Not to the boy who's playing Jim's part here, nor to a Jim

who, when he's out of school, broods nostalgically over its smells and noises, but to an active Jim, living in school and learning there crafty ways of getting round the rules which he has himself laid down and which he accepted when he first passed inside the school doors. If you don't stick to your role, we shall never get anywhere; you must play the game properly.'

'I've never been more serious. Is it true that I spoke in my own name rather than in Jim's? Can't Jim be sensitive to smells and noises?'

'Suppose he were, we'd ask him to leave that out of account, since as you admitted yourself all that belongs to the past, and we agreed that Jim should speak only about the present. As you were! Jim shall stand in front of George, who'll be his teacher, and let's listen to the conversation between master and pupil.'

'Well now, since you admit that you're in the wrong, will you tell me why you have got yourself into this position?'

'Er, I don't know, sir. . . .'

'You don't know? Little liar! For that you deserve to have your punishment doubled!'

'I didn't do it on purpose, sir.'

'That's a well-worn excuse from a schoolboy! If I were not in fact aware that you did it on purpose, I should merely have informed you that you were being punished and I should not insist on your telling me why you have incurred this well-deserved punishment.'

'One can't always keep the rules, sir.'

"I grant you it's not easy, I grant you that, but do you expect me to be satisfied with such an answer? I don't like your

smile, upon my word, it looks as if you were flouting me! Am
I going to have to pull your ears?'

'By all means, sir, do that, it's your job.'

'Impertinent boy! But I refuse to be upset my your insolence. Let us assume that I did not hear that remark. Well,
why have you misbehaved?'

'In order to let you do your job, sir.'

'Another piece of impertinence, and you are still evading
my question!'

'I'm not evading it, any more than I mean to be impertinent.
I answered your questions as best I could, sir.'

'Was it in order to give me an excuse for punishing you that
you made yourself liable to punishment?'

'Oh, you are merely a tool, sir.'

'A tool? Worse and worse! A tool of which you make use
as you please, a tool intended to regulate your behaviour, and
whose efficiency you wanted to test, is that it?'

'That's about it, sir.'

'Oh, that's the limit! Leave the room, please!'

'Hurrah! What a fine scene, and how well acted!'

'So well that you fancied George himself to be choking with
indignation!'

'And that you expected him to break into the conversation
himself!'

'Were you speaking for the pupil and the master as well?'

'Yes, but it was George who inspired the master's remarks,
which you thought you heard coming from his lips.'

'So George can't be said to have remained silent.'

'But he can't be held to have spoken, either. He would only
have opened his lips to express the master's anger, not his own.

Where's the difference between saying a lesson and acting a part? So George has remained faithful to his vow.'

'I wonder if George admits that one can open one's lips and yet remain silent.'

'His silence proves that he doesn't admit it.'

'After all, what we learn from this scene is that the masters' authority is weak, their influence negligible.'

'Not quite, for although it's likely that if we were freed from our masters' supervision we should keep the rules just the same, it must be admitted that the awe they inspire gives substance to these rules. And then, when the cat's away, the mice will play, we know, but if the cat were to grant them an eternal respite, would they go on playing or would they go to sleep from the sheer boredom of their security? We have no sense of security, we have to be always on guard, to be continually scheming. That's the theme we shall ask Jim to develop for us, with reference to the school's over-loaded time-table. You'll see from that that everything has been worked out by our masters with a view to keeping us on the alert. Anyone who gets behind in his time-table, out of laziness or presumption, will pay for it with the loss of his liberty until evening. But now listen to Jim.'

Now the actor playing Jim speaks with Paul's voice, in the stupidly mechanical manner of a young rustic, as indifferent to the substance of his lesson as to the tone on which it should be recited:

'From the moment the bell wakes us, harried by the need to be out of bed, washed and dressed before the supervisor's whistle summons us to fall into line and go to our daily work, these practical tasks with which our day begins are important only in so far as they make us conform to rule, and spare us the shame of being called to order by the authority whose right to supervise and correct us we acknowledge. We wash with scrupulous care under the critical eye of the master only to avoid being scolded by him for neglecting our toilet.'

'But then. . . . Allow me to interrupt Jim for a moment. . . . But then, should the master relax his vigilance, you'd relax your zeal too, and that implies that but for the fear of being scolded, you'd give up those rules of hygiene which you consider restrictions on your liberty, and that implies a paradoxical argument in the masters' favour.'

'Jim isn't making himself clear. If these duties were not imposed on us by the masters, it's obvious that we should not strive to perform them well in the masters' presence and badly in their absence. We should just perform them !'

'Decidedly, I am less and less convinced of the usefulness of masters !'

'Don't you understand that the masters have made something dramatic out of the rules by giving the character of a permanent conflict to our relations with them, which have taken the place of the rules? It's the masters whom we have to obey, it's they who punish us and whom, consequently, we are tempted to disobey so as to enable them, in our pupil's impertinent phrase, to *do their job.* By surreptitiously resisting their orders, by outwitting their vigilance in order to incur a well-deserved punishment, we avoid being lulled into self-satisfied docility, but at the same time we admit the invincible power of those rules, whose very existence depends on the frequency of our offences. And indeed the masters themselves invite us to commit these offences by reminding us of our duties and by unceasingly threatening us with penalties. But let Jim speak again.'

'And if we strive to learn the lessons and write the exercises set by our masters the day before, it's solely in order to win those good marks which, by satisfying their requirements, ensure our safe exemption from punishment. Similarly, when we're careless and inattentive, it's merely to strengthen within ourselves the sense of bondage, not to cast it off. So, when the master chooses to make an example of us for the benefit of our more timid companions, we shall serve our sentence without feeling the mortified fury of the defeated, and without uttering a protest, since our illicit chatter had no other object than to incur punishment.'

'But excuse me, isn't there a risk of eventually mistaking the masters for the rules, and the rules for the masters?'

'In so far as the masters have usurped all the functions they assume. But in the masters' opinion we should have run other risks by escaping from their tutelage, for without the infamous blackmail to which they subject us, without the obligations they impose on us, without the series of punishments they inflict on us for any breach of discipline, the rules would lose their very name, and from the fact that we could no longer name them....'

'They would cease to exist, of course! Whence it follows that your submission to these blackmailing masters is the surest guarantee of your submission to the rules?'

'That's enough, Paul, that's enough! We're getting fed up with your Jim and your rules and your masters.'

'All right. Let's give up talking about the rules.'

'No, Paul, you'd better say: let's give up trying to make George talk! Admit your failure, confess that you'd hoped

to make George speak by subjecting him, like the rest of us,
to the ordeal of your tiresome sophistry, but George endured
it without speaking a word, even if for a moment he seemed
to fall in with your game, during that picturesque schoolroom
scene in which you'd cast him in the role of the schoolmaster,
which he only played by making faces! Admit your mistake,
Paul! Now let's condemn George to endure our silence and
you'll see that he, in his turn, will lose patience and he will try
to break it, and will only succeed by renouncing his own
silence!'

'Now George has been warned! How can he lose at a game
where you rashly spread all the cards out in front of him?'

'So because I take little account of your paltry tricks, of the
two obvious traps in your elaborate speeches, I'm going to lose
the game? How naïve to believe that my remarks could
strengthen George's position, when yours were unable to drive
him from it! We have seen the fine result of your learned
dissertations on the subject—and why not, after all?—of your
school rules, we've seen them spinning aimlessly round and
then breaking off short in front of George, who's perfectly
self-possessed—the more boring for us!'

'All right. Then it's up to you to tell us the rules of this new
game.'

'The game is the same, except that the parts will now be
reversed and it'll be George's job to make us talk.'

'I doubt whether he'll consent, now that Paul's unfortunate
attempt has made him wise!'

'And we've learned this evening that George preferred silent
roles!'

'And will you tell me who'll be proclaimed the winner,

George who'll have got us to speak by speaking to us, or we who'll have got him to speak by not speaking to him?'

'You have to understand that if George has refused to communicate with us when we mistakenly used speech as a weapon against his muteness, it's because he found it easy to meet our chatter with muteness, but who, for any length of time, could silently endure the company of the silent, except in a community where to keep silence is the rule? Now this room has never, except in fancy, been the place where the rules hold sway! Why all this talk of traps, restrictions, resistance and defeat? I say that when George breaks silence it will be in full awareness and as though driven by some irresistible impulse, in order to make us break our silence; I say that we could not accuse him of breaking his vow, since he would only renounce it on condition of joining with us in an exchange of fraudulent words of which we should all be dupes. We're not going to wring his first word from him, this time, by means of some guileful demonstration, it must spring spontaneously from his silence as an appeal to our own silence, as heartrending as a prayer, as urgent as a cry from the heart!'

'Listen to him, listen to him! How boring this is going to be! After having had to endure Paul's stodgy lectures, now we're ordered to keep silence!'

'How long shall we be able to keep a straight face, I wonder?'

'If you feel like laughing, who's going to stop you?'

'Shall we be allowed to amuse ourselves? I was going to propose a game of draughts to Paul, but should we be able to play it in silence?'

'We might ask George to display his talent for mimicry, we'll be the audience....'

'You'd do better to realise that we're not here to have fun.'

'I fancy I'd realised that!'

'Yes, I think Paul undertook to make that quite clear!'

'There's someone here who's offended by your jokes.'

'D'you mean George? It looks as if he were drinking in every word we speak.'

'Every word you speak drives him deeper into silence. If that's what you're aiming at. . . .'

'It's true that we're not being serious, but that's by way of preparation for too much seriousness.'

'It's healthy to relax after school and before settling down to prep!'

'Yes, it really seems as if we were in that school Jim described; Paul's our teacher, and here is our supervisor!'

'In that case, your supervisor now blows his whistle for the end of break and orders you to shut up!'

'Then we're now to be at the mercy of some whim of George's and we're not to speak again unless he speaks to us?'

'O Saint George the Silent! Help us in our misfortune! We had the power of speech and it's been withdrawn from us because we misused it, and it's for you to restore it to us, amen, so be it!'

'George's smile implies that he is not unmoved by our prayer.'

'Enough nonsense! If only you'd behave properly at last. . . .'

'If we did so, we should prevent you from doing your job, to borrow that impertinent phrase of Jim's which Paul so aptly quoted and which I quote in my turn to show that I've profited by the lesson.'

'You've understood it quite wrong! You forget that we are not in school here....'

'Is that really so? Everything this evening proves to me that we are!'

'Then you'd better look out! For if you were right, I should be entitled as your master to send you out of the room for inattention and chattering! But really, aren't you tired of talking without saying anything?'

'Never tired enough to shut up, always too tired to say something!'

'Is it beyond your power to behave as if you were bound to keep silence for ever?'

'All right! We'll imitate George, who doesn't find it beyond his power.'

'And you shall have your reward! Remember what I tell you : George will speak, George will save us all!'

Just as he could not have left his post so long as the children's voices could be heard behind the door, so now he feels fascinated to the point of dizziness by their muteness and he shares with them their hope of deliverance, which will be his deliverance as well. Each of them has spoken on his behalf, but it is as if he himself had spoken for each of them with a vehemence that he considers disproportionate with the insignificance of that extravagant colloquy, which was probably only a subtle parody of the teachers' pretentious verbosity. Now that the children have ceased to speak, it is as if he himself had renounced speech, but then his presence behind the door has no purpose and seems motivated solely by the imminence of some dénouement. Nevertheless, far from feeling himself frustrated by the children's muteness, he would have considered himself, as it were, admitted to take part in their game himself, were it not that this silence, by swallowing up the very memory of their words, has only ceased to be the children's silence in order to become his own. Thus it will be for him alone to face it and break it, to ensure their safety as well as his own— and not for that George who, by sharing their lot, has lost the benefit of his muteness which he owed only to their speech. The silence confronts him now like a formidable aggressor, to whom each moment adds strength. A silence which soon grows so voluminous that it seems about to burst the narrow space of the room in which it is confined, a silence as heavy and blank as rising anger. And should it be himself, the prying witness, whom the children were putting to the test of silence in order to deride him and force him to unmask himself, should they be still keeping watch behind that door, he could not make sure of it without falling into their trap. But as for his own presence, of which he is already doubtful, how can he affirm it except by proclaiming it at the top of his lungs? For is he in fact really there, is he still in the passage where silence sets his temples throbbing like the startled murmur of his blood?

'Are you there, children?' he cries, flinging himself against the door in a frenzied movement. 'Are you still there?'

Then he came to himself, and remembered joyfully that his name was George. Opening his eyes, he saw the boy Paul burst into his room. He saw him bend close to his ear to inform him with a smile that someone wanted to speak to him downstairs.

'To speak to me, did you say, my boy? To speak to me?'

And as he was hurriedly getting up, he saw the child smile to him again, but the smile was remote and enigmatic.

THE GREAT MOMENTS OF
A SINGER

THE GREAT MOMENTS OF A SINGER

HAVING HEARD his voice on only two occasions out of the twenty on which it proved to be the finest of this century, I shall not attempt to explain here the amazing phenomenon which suddenly, though for a brief period only, enabled an obscure performer to command so extraordinarily wide a compass that he could accomplish unprecedented feats of vocal acrobatics, such as bridging with ease the largest intervals, soaring or sinking to the most inaccessible notes, or, according to the requirements of his role, taking the bass, baritone or tenor part at will. It has been suggested that this singer's throat may have been the seat of an organic disturbance, possibly of cellular nature, which endowed it with exceptional elasticity until the final reabsorption of the disease. The hypothesis is a far-fetched one, although I have heard the singer himself give it his approval; yet even if it should provide a physiological explanation of this curious case, many other puzzles remain unsolved, such as, in the first place : how did it happen that his interpretations of Don Giovanni, Otello or Caspar proved so rich and so convincing as to eclipse those which his far more experienced predecessors, whose fame has been more lasting, had given of the same parts? Might it be said, in reply to this, that a disease is liable not merely to attack an organism but to spread into all regions of the nervous system, sometimes acting as a discharge upon a hitherto amorphous nature and awakening almost superhuman faculties in an artist of only mediocre talent?

But I do not propose to review the various solutions that have been offered to the problem of this brief career; they are all quite unworthy of its impressive and enigmatic character, and their authors, while proving incapable of providing any technical explanation of the prodigious virtues of this voice, have moreover neglected, in their study of the phenomenon, that of the personality of the artist himself, whom I was privileged to know during a critical period of his private life. But first, for a proper understanding of what is to come, it is essential to recall briefly the circumstantial details of his dizzy ascent to fame.

Frédéric Molieri, whose father was an Italian wine merchant in Bologna and whose mother was a Frenchwoman, at an early age showed a keen interest in the theatre, which he frequented without the knowledge of his parents, who rightly or wrongly reproached him for indolence and frivolity. As sometimes happens to highly gifted children who have been badly directed and are apathetic by nature, he did nothing to develop his aptitudes, and, whether from lack of courage or from thoughtlessness, he did not even try to make contact with the actors whom he applauded every evening, relying for everything on chance rather than on his personal efforts—a fatalistic attitude which explains many circumstances of his life and even his indifference in face of failure. On the request of his parents, who naïvely sought to divert him from a passion which they considered detrimental to his studies, one of his uncles, a violin-maker by profession, taught him to play the violin and the oboe. Two years later he was accepted as a member of a local orchestra where, according to the works on the programme, he played both these instruments in turn, with a marked preference for the second, at which he soon excelled.

It is unnecessary to recall here all the stages of his career as instrumentalist, which was honourable but deliberately modest. He would never consent to appear in public except amid the anonymous crowd of performers, repeatedly refusing with significant stubborness to perform as soloist or in any smaller group of players where he would have been more or less conspicuous, and this reluctance to put himself forward makes plausible, if not convincing, the theory that he was holding himself in reserve, warned by a sort of premonition, for the day when through some unexpected stroke of luck he would be able suddenly to reveal to an astonished audience his mastery of an art which no one had hitherto seen him practise—except for one single person who, as we shall see, played a part in this affair.

A few years later we find him in Frankfort, a member of one of the most famous orchestras of Europe, on the eve of accomplishing his amazing feat. After this everything happened like a third-rate film scenario. The programme of the orchestra to which he belonged included for this tour, besides a series of concerts, alternating performances of *Don Giovanni* and *The Magic Flute*. It is interesting to note that Molieri sought, and was granted by the producer, the privilege of appearing on the stage among the musicians who, wearing make-up, costumes and wigs like real actors, perform at Don Giovanni's party at the end of the first act. We must note moreover that never before this day had he put forward such a request.

Shortly before the opening chords of the overture, some

anxiety was caused by the absence of the leading interpreter; someone was sent to look for him and presently brought him back, to the great relief of the producer, who had neglected to provide the usual understudy. In the general bustle that precedes the rise of the curtain, nobody noticed the actor's peculiar manner and dishevelled appearance as he was hustled into his dressing-room. Nobody wondered at the suspicious blotches on his livid face, which powder and paint were fortunately to disguise. And it was a high-spirited Don Giovanni, a fiery seducer who appeared on the stage up till the end of the act. It is important to recall here that all those who had the good fortune to witness this memorable performance agree that the Viennese singer surpassed himself both in vocal purity and in dramatic power. However, perhaps to revenge themselves on him for having subsequently been the victims of a somewhat mortifying hoax, certain spectators criticised him for the almost embarrassing realism with which he acted the part of a man excited by wine and sensual pleasure, for falsifying the import of the drama by exaggerating the element of frenzy in the character—a licentious nobleman, but a proud one, who should maintain his self-control even in debauchery. The conductor laughingly complained of the breakneck speed set by the singer who, carried away by his excitement and as though in a state of trance, particularly in the later scenes, played his part without taking any notice of the beat, as if he had completely forgotten where he was and tried to evade the responsibilities of his role.

But what can Frédéric Molieri, the most privileged of all the spectators by reason of his position on the stage and his profound knowledge of the score, have thought of the liberties unjustifiably taken by the famous singer? Did he discern something suspicious about the exaggerated gestures, painfully suggestive of a drunken man staggering out of a tavern, and in that case may one suppose that he foresaw the disaster and calculated the advantage to be gained from it? We cannot say, but it is just as likely that, with no ulterior motive, he appreciated the originality of an interpretation which in many respects resembled that which he was shortly to make his own : perhaps he had no inkling of what was to come.

One cannot resist conjecture about what seems to us in retrospect to have been a crucial moment in his career from the fact that we know how soon it was to be followed by his electrifying début. On the balcony where he had just taken part in the performance of the famous minuet, Molieri was presumably very far from suspecting that he was about to take the decisive step, and when the curtain fell on Don Giovanni standing amidst the disordered remains of the festivities, not in the splendid attitude of a freethinker defying heaven's thunderbolts, but in that of a guilty and defeated man—thus anticipating events and depriving his character of its heroic dimension—perhaps then he discovered with stupefaction that the singer had stopped acting, perhaps the thunderclaps that punctuate the closing bars echoed in his ears like an invitation to try his luck. . . .

Hardly had the curtain fallen when Don Giovanni tottered into the arms of Leporello and Don Ottavio, who helped him to his dressing-room, where he collapsed, uttering a stream of abuse against the authors of a criminal assault of which he declared himself victim. The doctor on duty was summoned, but the singer repulsed him with an angry gesture and stag-

gered as best he could on to the stage, where he had to acknowledge the acclamations of the audience. Recalled for the
third time, he blew kisses to every corner of the house with the
engaging shamelessness of a *café-concert* star; and apparently
he was unaware of the unfortunate impression he made, for
now in a supreme effort he flung out his arms as though to
clutch an enormous ball, bent his knees and was doubtless
about to indulge in some fresh extravagance when the fall of
the curtain cut short, once and for all, this deplorable exhibition.

A moment later he lay slumped in an arm-chair with eyes
half closed and quivering lips, replying to the urgent questions
of those around him only by invective interspersed with sobs.
What had happened exactly? The rumour went around that
he was drunk when he went on to the stage, but nobody could
testify directly to having seen him in a state of inebriation that
night, and moreover he was not given to such indulgence, even
accidentally; the bruises discovered on his face, when his
make-up was removed, would have given credibility to his
own story, according to which he had been accosted and
brutally manhandled by unknown persons in the street, had
not the stubborn way he evaded all questions about this sup-
posed assault, and his refusal to lay any complaint, made it
more than suspect. But the true causes of his collapse are of
little importance to us; what interests us here is that despite all
the producer's entreaties he declared himself unable to sustain
his role to the end and insisted on the doctor's immediately
providing a certificate of unfitness.

We can imagine the despair of the producer, faced with the
choice of entrusting the part at a moment's notice to some

unprepared singer (but to whom? who would dare assume such an honour, coupled with such risk?) or of refunding the tickets after a personal apology to his dissatisfied audience. As occasionally happens in time of crisis, when any action involves its author's responsibility, instead of calmly reflecting on the best way of solving the problem, the producer listened to the advice lavished on him by all and sundry without making up his mind to follow any of it; the interval was almost over and he was still wondering what decision to take, while the whole company was grumbling about this incident which might seriously jeopardise the success of their tour. It was then that one of the violinists who, having also been a member of the little stage band, was still wearing his fine silk costume, came timidly up to the stage manager : 'What about Molieri?'

'Molieri?' asked the stage manager. 'And who's Molieri?'

'One of the oboists in the orchestra, but a marvellous singer too.'

'Molieri? Are you making fun of me?'

'No, sir, indeed not!' And the violinist described how he had been taking a walk along the banks of the Main the previous day with Molieri, when the latter had suddenly hidden behind a bush to sing some passages from *Don Giovanni*, faithfully mimicking now the voice of L——, the singer who had collapsed, and now that of N——, who that very evening was playing Leporello.

'It was amazing, sir! I thought I'd gone crazy!'

The same reaction was felt a few moments later by all those —musicians, actors, walkers-on, stage hands—who were aware of the substitution, and it was thus expressed by those members of the audience who learned that it was not the famous L——

whom they had just been applauding after the last act, but some unknown last-minute understudy : 'Nonsense! what are you talking about? Of course it was him! it was the same man! We aren't crazy!'

The violinist who had saved the situation by suggesting to the producer an appeal to Molieri, although he had already experienced the day before an impression similar to that we have described, was rivetted to the spot when he saw Molieri come into the office to which he had been hastily summoned. The prestige invariably conferred on the mildest of individuals by his disguise, on an actor by his mask, on a priest by his vestments, played no part in the disturbing impression felt by the violinist at the sight of Molieri, who in all probability had already put off his splendid stage costume and was wearing the sombre dinner-jacket compulsory for players in the orchestra pit. He was struck by the proud, ecstatic expression of the man whose modesty he had always appreciated, and this metamorphosis was all the more hallucinating in that it also affected precise physical details such as the man's height or the colour of his eyes : although he was shorter than the average he seemed to tower over everyone and his face, which was in no way remarkable (as I can bear witness), had the radiance of a bright sun.

Taking into account the supremely unreal, make-believe atmosphere behind the scenes, one may suppose that the violinist was subconsciously influenced by that future fame which he alone foresaw, and which for him shed its glory beforehand on Molieri's whole person; perhaps he already saw him as he was to appear that very evening to thousands of spectators, willing victims of the same mirage, in fact as each of them was henceforward to imagine the figure of the law-defying seducer. (Actually the reverse impression—disappointment instead of delighted wonder—is what we sometimes feel when we see at close quarters, mingling with the crowd like anyone else, some actor of rather commonplace appearance whom, thanks to the aid of footlights, costume and the fiction of which he was the hero, we had set in a privileged world and invested with an almost divine grandeur. When I was introduced to Molieri I experienced a similar sense of disquiet : what had this man in common with the demoniacal character whom I had seen on the stage, struck down by death's thunderbolt ?)

After a hasty audition in which, according to witnesses, Molieri gave only a tolerable performance (but indeed what amateur would have acquitted himself more honourably ?) the producer took the risk of entrusting him with the principal role. When the curtain fell he clasped him in his arms, weeping with enthusiasm, and the very next day offered him a contract which Molieri was at first reluctant to sign, declaring that he was by no means sure of being able to repeat his exploit; these scruples were attributed to artistic vanity whereas, in my opinion, they sprang from a quite legitimate prudence : how can one commit oneself to giving something one does not possess and which is liable to fail one at any moment ?

II

Although I was never in any way an intimate friend of Molieri's, my limited acquaintance with him has subsequently suggested a number of reflections on the problem raised by his

case, and I feel justified in rejecting any interpretation of it
which conflicts with the few remarks I have heard him make
in my presence. It was during a visit to London that I happened, in quick succession, to see him on the stage for the first
time and then to be introduced to him by a mutual friend, a
woman of whom I had lost sight for many years and whom
I met by chance in the following circumstances. The business
affair for which I had undertaken this journey in the depths
of winter having been concluded after four hours' palaver in a
third-rate restaurant, amid clouds of cigar smoke, I had slipped
out to take a turn in the streets, in a sullen mood caused by
the feeling of having been cheated during the discussion in
which I had had to partake in my extremely rudimentary
English, joined to the impression of insecurity I am apt to experience when I go about by myself in a foreign town. In spite
of the mist, which was only apparent if one looked up at the
sky where a pale, gelatinous sun was floating, every outline
and moulding of the houses stood out with startling sharpness,
as in stormy weather at the seaside, but the dark red colour
characteristic of certain London buildings, far from brighten-
ing this poverty-stricken neighbourhood, only made it seem
more sinister. In front of me the street ran down into a tiled
tunnel over which a railway passed; this underground passage,
adequately lit on either side by a double chain of lamps fixed
in the walls, without offering any definite threat, promptly
inspired me with a panic wish to turn back. It seemed to me
just then that I should incur a great risk by plunging into that
tunnel. Instead of obeying my first impulse I hurried on,
anxious above all to emerge as fast as possible on the other
side, but scarcely had I stepped under the vault than I was

deafened by a din which made me lose all my self-control, and I began to run, shouting at the top of my voice, my eyes fixed on the semi-circular exit in which I could see framed two figures of identical height apparently coming to meet me, on the same pavement as myself. Shortly before I came level with them I resumed my natural pace, my head still awhirl with the metallic clangour (or with my own cries?), panting like a dog in the sun, but quite calm again and even ashamed of my cowardice. The two strangers—a man and a woman— stared curiously at me as we passed each other. I did not need to turn round to guess that they were looking back at me and probably exchanging ironic comments on my behaviour. Then I heard a delighted voice calling me; my name rang out in gradually decreasing echoes all along the deep gallery, and I saw the woman running towards me; this time I recognised her as an old friend, a very dear friend, Anna Fercovitz. It was the same narrow face, the same sparkling eyes and the tender, mischievous smile I had known of old.

'It's you!' she cried breathlessly, taking my hand and clasping it in her own, her eyes raised to my face as if she were in doubt of my reality. 'What a fright you gave us! And it's you!'

My ears were still buzzing, I could not hear her distinctly, or was it the reverberation that blurred her voice? I smiled stupidly without replying. She shook me by the elbow, crying that we must meet again at all costs. Then she rummaged busily in her handbag and drew out a pink ticket which she pressed between my fingers: 'Here you are. You've got to come, by hook or by crook. We'll have a good talk afterwards.' She fastened her bag again and gave me a friendly smile, as

though she had cast off a grave responsibility. I saw her go
back to take her companion's arm and hurry him off, gesticula-
ting with her gloved hand in her old petulant manner, which
still delighted me today. But why such haste? She had vanished as quickly as she had appeared before me. Was it from
tact that she had assumed so excitable a manner? Or to drive
away the shame of accidentally seeing what she would doubtless rather not have seen? I waited till I was out of the tunnel
—a fresh train passed meanwhile, but this time I experienced
only a slight irritation—to examine by daylight the ticket she
had slipped into my hand.

Excited in anticipation, as in the far off days of my childhood, by the thrill of delight I always feel at watching an opera,
even when the spectacle is not of a high standard, while that
of the musical interpretation, about which I am more exacting,
was guaranteed by the reputation of the theatre, I made my
way to Covent Garden, where the work to be performed was
one which, without ever having seen it on the stage before, I
immediately included among my favourites, possibly because
of the mysteriously romantic associations of its title and its
author : *Der Freischütz* by Carl-Maria von Weber.

Anna was not the only occupant of the box to which she
had invited me. Three gentlemen in evening dress were sitting
with her. They all rose to welcome me, but Anna made no
attempt to introduce me to her companions, to whom she did
not speak a word throughout the evening, as if they had only
been there to wait on her, and indeed this appeared to be their
function. They would pass her the opera glasses, or help her to
put on her fur cape, and their assiduous rivalry involved a
certain amount of confusion. At the end of each act they would

applaud profusely, but neither more nor less than Anna (which is to say far more than any other spectator); they obviously only shared in her enthusiasm out of pure politeness. I ended by paying no more attention to these strange gentlemen than if they had been servants. To the few words I whispered in her ear—how glad I was to see her again, how little she had changed, etc.—she replied monosyllabically, with the inattentive, preoccupied air of someone who finds conversation a nuisance; it did not take me long to realise that she would have preferred to see me behave with the same rather stiff reserve as the three gentlemen. As I watched her profile, while the first bars of the famous overture rang out, I discovered about her features something altered which gave the lie to the compliment I had just paid her : she could not master a certain nervous tension, which scored painful lines about her mouth; she was still beautiful, but it seemed as if she had utterly lost confidence in the power that every woman derives from awareness of her beauty. More precisely, this seemed an unimportant card in the game that she had to play. But this reflection—and certain others I shall mention—may only have occurred to me much later, when I realised that her tense and anxious expression betrayed certain difficulties in her private life connected with the theatre itself.

It needs the powerful genius of Weber, interpreted by artists of high quality—it needs the sovereign ease of their voices, the vividness of their acting—to turn this libretto, derived from a simple and rather silly legend, into the savage drama that impresses us as the projection of our most elementary feelings —our terrors, our hallucinations. No subsequent interpretation has ever seemed to me to bring out so clearly the element

of doom that marks the character of Caspar, generally considered a secondary figure, to which the actor who played it
that evening had restored all its sombre grandeur and its
sinister power, never had this puerile tale of huntsmen and
witchcraft—which is merely the background for fine romantic
music—been clothed for me with so much mystery. From the
loud rifle shot which opens the first act to the final scene of
reconciliation, everything seemed to take place on a super-
natural plane, the lively or gently pastoral episodes seemed
steeped in a shadowy fairy atmosphere and even the somewhat insipid passages that are unfortunately redolent of the
taste of the time seemed to benefit by the moonlight colours
of the whole thing. But the person who really gave life to this
fantastic spectacle, and from whom I could never take my eyes
when he was on the stage, was the marvellous singer who
played the part of Caspar, the forester who has sold himself
to the Devil according to the libretto, but whom everything
about this interpretation made one take for the Devil in person.
With a boldness for which he was often criticised later, the
singer, refusing to bow to the crude romantic law of contrasts,
had accomplished the remarkable feat of uniting in a single
tragic style the most antithetical elements, and of communica-
ting to all the protagonists of the drama that sombre and
frenzied energy which kept them, from beginning to end, at
an extreme pitch of incandescence; overriding any concern
for the picturesque, he freed the tale from its too narrowly
anecdotal character and raised it to the level of myth; it is
remarkable that even those scenes in which Caspar does not
appear were affected by his infernal presence. If it is true that
this interpretation falsified the general import of the work

by subordinating everything to the demoniacal element and passing too lightly over the others—gaiety, sentiment, pathos —no member of the audience was in a condition to decide this, for the spell that bound them all made them incapable, for a long time, of any objective judgment. I have said that all the voices were beyond reproach, but on hearing Caspar's even the most frivolous listeners, those who were least sensitive to the power of song, must have felt themselves touched to the heart and as it were rapt out of themselves.

To return to Anna, the interest she took in the performance had the curious effect of detaching her from the prevailing emotion; she may perhaps only have been paying particularly close attention, and this unremitting effort to let nothing escape her gave her an axious look, that of a woman of no definite age asking a question of the utmost importance without ever receiving the answer she desires. Even the prolonged applause with which she greeted the performers at the end of each act had something ostentatious about it, which made one doubt whether she was joining sincerely in the general enthusiasm. 'What do you think of Molieri?' she asked, turning to me, and that was how I learnt the name of the fabulous singer. Without waiting for my answer, and as though it was not of the slightest interest to her, she immediately added with puerile pride : 'A great singer, yes indeed. He is my lover.'

I did not know at the time that she was lying, and that was why everything about her announcement surprised me, her almost provocative shamelessness, her vanity (the last fault to be expected from a woman so modest, so devoid of coquetry) and even the somewhat stilted expression which I believe she used without a hint of irony.

K

'I congratulate you. He's really very fine,' I said politely.

'Fine, did you say?' she asked me with sudden agitation, and urged me to express myself more clearly: did I mean he was a fine-looking man? I began to laugh; a fine-looking man, most certainly. She grasped my arm: 'But tell me, was that what you thought the first time, the very first time, when you saw him in the street?' And when I replied that I had never seen him before that evening, she seemed dismayed. Our conversation lapsed. She asked me to take her into the foyer, but no sooner were we in the passage than she gave me the slip, deliberately I am sure, for I saw her thread her way through the crowd, making no attempt to turn round and beckon me to follow her. Somewhat mortified, I lost sight of her until the end of the interval, when I found her sitting in the box, once again very taciturn.

I cannot attempt to describe the rest of the performance, which was so strange and so moving that I quite forgot to watch Anna: in that famous scene in the Wolf's Glen Molieri brought out, with an extraordinary note of truth, something which is usually confined, as it were, within a somewhat preposterous nightmare. I felt driven by an imperious secret power, carried away by this voice which came straight and unaltered from another world.

Anna, who had risen when the actors were recalled for the last time, glanced at me with puzzled eyes, blinking, as one does on meeting somebody one has not seen for a long time or has never expected to see again. It was humilating, but had she not read in my own eyes the same bewildered stupefaction? As she walked past me she called out in a lively tone: 'Well now, let's go to supper!' and I heard the solemn voices of the three gentlemen chorusing assent, after which they began to argue confusedly all the way down the stairs and even in the street. Anna, whose arm I had taken, whispered contemptuously in my ear: 'Listen to them! Always finding fault, the idiots!' Refusing to let me take her to a restaurant of my own choice, she hurried us into a milk bar adjoining the theatre, where she peremptorily ordered a modest pot of tea. Had we really come there to 'have a good talk' under the eyes of those three 'idiots'? Before realising that she was waiting for somebody (yet she was obviously on the *qui vive*), I endeavoured vainly to draw her from her taciturnity, and my mood grew increasingly sombre. When the tea was brought, we drank it in silence.

A moment later she introduced me to Frédéric Molieri, whom I found, to my keen disappointment, to be a very commonplace little man with a shy look and rather stiff gestures. 'We've scarcely met,' he said, shaking my hand in friendly fashion, and broke into a somewhat vulgar laugh as if he had made a good joke, but his face was quite unfamiliar to me, and it was only when Anna remarked: 'Oh, we were in such a hurry that I never thought of introducing you, besides it was hardly a suitable place!' that I realised to what he was alluding; to cut short any embarrassing question, I confessed that I had not recognised him on the stage, although I had scarcely taken my eyes off him throughout the performance (but this also implied that without Anna's introduction I should not have recognised him in the milk bar either). I could see that my words had cast a certain chill over the atmosphere and I went on rather clumsily to offer compliments which he accepted with a pained frown. He raised a hand to silence me, and looked at me reproachfully: 'How tired I feel!' he muttered to himself, passing his hand over his face. 'Tired, tired to death!' There was indeed a remarkable contrast between the overflowing vitality he displayed on the stage and his present weariness, emphasised by his puny appearance. It seemed as if he had concentrated all his strength into his song, that all energy that did not serve his singing had gone out of him. In the theatre his voice had had a tonic quality; here it was neutral, lifeless, fixed in dreary apathy.

I remember little about that evening that is worth relating. Anna and Molieri—and occasionally the three gentlemen—talked with a frivolous inconsequence that left my expectations continually disappointed. I wondered whether it was my presence that made them deliberately avoid any serious topic: their futile conversation protected them from my justifiable curiosity. But one thing I have not forgotten and shall never forget: the savage, really brutal gesture with which Molieri shook off Anna's hand as she laid it on his. His eyes darkened with disgust, his face was distorted in an expression of outraged horror. Anna did not show the most fleeting sign of having been thus publicly affronted. Everything went on as if her gesture and Molieri's had been unimportant, implying no threat, without significance for herself or for him. To break the tension I begged Molieri to explain certain obscure passages in the drama whose hero he had just played; he affected utter ignorance, and declared with a humble smile that he had never studied that idiotic libretto; to sing his role in German he had learnt it by heart without understanding a single word: 'I just indulged in the pleasure of singing,' he confessed.

'And yet,' I said, 'you *were* Caspar, you *were* the accursed huntsman!'

'Pooh! A trumpery devil, far less destructive than Don Giovanni, although Don Giovanni himself isn't very wicked. . . .' And he complained of the poverty of the operatic repertoire, where one might seek in vain for a male character who is at once the instrument and the victim of evil. (Another time, I remember, he instanced Carmen and Alban Berg's Lulu as the only two roles he would have liked to play. 'And what's to stop you from playing either of them?' Anna then protested jokingly.) The rest of the evening was spent discussing trivial professional incidents, health worries and other unimportant matters which I have not remembered.

Anna Fercovitz rang me up next morning at my hotel, and to my surprise reproached me for my unfriendly manner the night before. Why so much reserve between two such old friends? She solemnly assured me that she had spent a sleepless night worrying about me. I returned her complaints in kind, with a certain petulance, but she reiterated them in the same tone, which was that of genuine resentment (and no one was less given to play-acting than she). After which, with equal sharpness and far more perspicacity, she accused me of disliking Molieri: 'You thought him insignificant, admit it! Utterly insignificant!' And she went on repeating the words, emphasing every syllable 'Utterly insignificant, didn't you?' I parried with the crudest platitude: so gifted an artist could not be insignificant, and this seemed to infuriate her: 'Listen, my dear fellow, Molieri himself, if he could hear you, would laugh in your face!' And I had the impression that Molieri was listening, and had in fact laughed.

I was flattered that she seemed to lay such store by my opinion, but I wondered anxiously whether she resented my

having confirmed her in her own, otherwise why so much
anger in her voice, why this oddly challenging tone? It really
seemed as if she had subjected me to an ordeal and that I had
come out of it very badly. Eventually we agreed on a new
rendezvous. But meanwhile I treated myself to an evening at
Covent Garden where Molieri was singing *Otello* in Italian :
this time he could not honestly pretend to be ignorant of the
meaning of his part, written in his native language. And yet
it was true that his voice, by virtue of an expressive power
which was almost miraculous, made words superfluous, while
the miming and gestures usually so essential to the understanding of the action of an opera seemed exaggerated. His voice
created an autonomous language, it was, here, the very language of jealousy. I shall refrain from discussing this performance, during which I felt my curiosity concerning Molieri
revive with almost painful sharpness. But having caught sight
during the interval of Anna leaning over the edge of the stage
box where we had sat together two nights before, I deliberately
avoided meeting her in the passages, in order not to expose myself after the performance to a fresh disappointment. And I
went back to my hotel in a state of excitement so violent that
I in my turn spent a sleepless night.

Next morning I reached our meeting-place a little before
the appointed time. Anna appeared a few minutes later, breathless, and with her face sketchily made-up. As we felt a certain
difficulty about opening the conversation, I proposed a short
walk in Hyde Park to conceal my embarrassment. But it was
in vain that I strove to interest her in our common recollections, in my affairs, in the events of my life, and just as I was
in despair of extracting from her the slightest confidence about

her own, she suddenly confessed, with lowered eyes, that she had at first intended to cut the rendezvous on which we had agreed.

'Sometimes, when one's very anxious to do something, you see, one mistrusts one's longing, one's afraid.'

'And you were very anxious to see me?'

'Very anxious, and very afraid. I've never had any secrets from you. You don't understand me,' she said with a smile. 'I want to talk to you and I'd rather not do so.'

We walked for a while in silence and the gravel of the path crunched under our feet. Then she asked me abruptly: 'What do you *really* think of Molieri?'

Somewhat disconcerted, I launched into the ambiguous generalisations that such a question seemed to call for. She interrupted me: 'You don't think anything of him, that's the truth!' and immediately added with unexpected violence: 'I shall have to leave him!'

Perhaps she felt the need to make this confession to me, but it was surely also in order to observe my reaction and get me to admit something which she suspected me of concealing from her. A little later, appalled by the silence which she had perfidiously allowed to settle between us, I uttered some ill-chosen words, the first that came into my head, the very words she was waiting for so as to reject them vehemently as being thoughtless and ill-founded. I had only a very superficial acquaintance with Molieri, which deprived my opinion of any importance, but how could I help being surprised to see her attracted to such a man?

'You dislike him?'

'I don't care for him very much, actually, but that's not the point.'

'What is the point, then?' she asked, defying me with her gaze.

'The point is that he doesn't care for you, and that I don't believe you care for him.'

'You're mistaken!' she cried with a note of vexation in her voice. 'If I didn't care for him. . . .' But she left her remark unfinished and, as if it mattered far more to her to have the reasons for my personal antipathy explained than to convince me of my error, she asked me, staring at me with piercing intensity: 'And why do you dislike Molieri?' I had to reply that I did not know, that it was not always easy to distinguish between one's instinct and one's reason, but she would not let me off: 'Is it because he doesn't talk much? But you have heard him sing!' she cried with a note of suffering in her voice that distressed me, although at the time her remark seemed to me quite devoid of meaning.

'I've heard him sing, yes indeed. And again last night.'

'You were there then!' she cried almost joyfully. 'So then you hadn't been disappointed!'

'Disappointed by such a wonderful voice?'

'Oh, his voice of course,' she murmured irritably, and I saw her hunch her shoulders with a dejected air, like someone who has given up trying to be understood. Nevertheless it was from that moment that our conversation took a more intimate turn: I remember that we questioned one another at length about what had become of the friends of our youth, and jokingly recalled the arguments we used to have together and the ludicrous circumstances in which we had known each other. However, we had already left the park some little time when she suddenly fell silent and, standing in front of me as if to prevent me from going any further, she exclaimed: 'No, you must not judge him hastily. You've got to see him again, you've got to talk to him! A noble voice, but a great heart too!'

Such a grandiloquent tone would have seemed unnatural in any other woman, but I knew Anna too well to think that it could be a trick intended to extort an emotional tribute from me. I took her hand: 'Calm down. Why are you afraid? You're laying too much store by my opinion, and in fact I've got none on the question that preoccupies you. So let's go on gossiping like a couple of old friends!' She cast a sombre glance over me: 'You've got no opinion? Well, that's just why I entreat you to come up with me!' And she pointed to a hotel in front of which she had led me, without my realising it and quite deliberately, as she frankly admitted later.

'Is that where you live?' But she answered neither yes nor no. 'You've got to see him,' she went on repeating with gentle obstinacy, thrusting me forcibly into the lift. She dragged me after her along the passages. She knocked at one door, then immediately afterwards at the next, which opened a crack to disclose the severe countenance of one of the three gentlemen, pressing his finger to his lips. The door closed again, and the first door behind us opened in its turn, while a solemn voice (I recognised it immediately) informed us that M. Molieri was not available. 'Not available?' Anna burst out laughing. 'Tell him who's come to see him!' There was a brief silence. 'I am very sorry, madame,' the voice replied firmly. 'M. Molieri is working and will see no visitors.' Anna turned to me, white and trembling. 'What impertinence!' she said, shrugging her shoulders. Then she flung herself against the door: 'Frédéric, it's me!' And the door opened to reveal Molieri, who shrank back with a sleepy grimace.

'What a row!' He looked at each of us in turn, and although he asked us to come in, the spite lurking in his eyes, the sly half-smile on his lips held us rooted to the spot. Anna evidently regretted having come; there stood this man in front of her, with a face about which there was absolutely nothing to say.

'We were just passing by,' she said in a miserable voice. 'But perhaps we're disturbing you?'

'Disturbing me? I'm always being disturbed,' he replied insolently, and then remarked to me: 'This good woman runs after me, what am I to do about it?'

I think this abominably vulgarity did not come naturally to him, I believe his fame had made him suspicious and he wanted to discourage any attempt at sympathy. I believe, moreover, that he felt extremely doubtful about Anna's feelings towards him and that these distressed him, as his feelings distressed her. But I found his cynicism revolting, and retorted curtly: 'In your place I should not complain of that.'

'You would surely have no reason to complain,' he replied with a smile, as if his own case were quite different. And he added immediately, to avoid any misunderstanding: 'No more than I should if I were irresistible.'

'Oh, but you are!' But I was thinking of Caspar and Otello, of whom this manikin in a dressing-gown was only a wretched caricature.

'Thank you, monsieur,' he said without a trace of irony or affectation. There was no personal feeling in the words, a meaningless mechanical 'thank you' uttered purely out of politeness, although politeness did not require it.

From the bathroom, whither he had retired to dress, he made clumsy jokes about the untimeliness of our visit, pretending to deplore the fact that Anna always came to badger him when he was at work and invariably failed to turn up when he could have spared her a little time. Anna scarcely replied, protested less and less and eventually lapsed into good-humoured laughter as if she really could not take these reproaches seriously. Whether because she was pleased with them, or because she could no longer endure the teasing tone in which they were uttered, she left the room surreptitiously, giving me to understand, as she went, that I was to stay. I now believe that she had chosen the best tactics for making Molieri alter his. And in fact, once he realised that she had gone, he stopped playing the fool.

'I see . . .' he said, casting his eye round the room. 'Do you think she's angry?'

'You teased her,' I said reproachfully.

'Not at all! I was speaking the truth. Your friend is very disconcerting. . . .'

'So are you!'

'Is it because I'm a very simple ordinary person?' he said, coming close to stare curiously at me. He could see that his perceptiveness had made me redden.

'That may be so,' I replied, dropping my eyes. 'But why do you delight in making her unhappy?'

'I make her unhappy?' he said in sincere amazement. 'Doesn't she rather make herself unhappy? She's an over-imaginative woman!' he added with a low laugh.

'No, I believe she has a strong affection for you. Does that make you laugh?'

He began walking slowly across the room : 'Listen to me : naturally, it distresses me very much to be loved for what I am not, but her case is worse : she cannot bring herself to hate me for what I am. It's a very difficult situation for her. Just remember that.'

'But that's a crazy notion !' I cried. 'Or else you're playing with words. If you could see her face while you're singing on the stage !'

'Yes, yes,' he said irritably. 'I tell you again : she cannot bring herself to hate me at other times, when I'm only a poor beggar. She's fallen for my voice. It's a difficult situation ! And now,' he said in a different voice, consulting his watch, 'that's enough talk.' He took off his dressing-gown and slipped on a jacket, slung a coat over his arm and came back to tell me, with an insincere smile : 'She left you alone with me here to get me to talk about what she'll ask you afterwards to repeat word for word. And that's what has happened.'

I protested that I had not come here to spy on him. He patted me on the shoulder : 'No, no, I said nothing of the sort. I like you very much. But stop worrying about Mme Fercovitz.' And he added something like : 'It all hangs by a thread !'

He persuaded me to walk with him to the studio close by, where he had a rehearsal, and on the way he never stopped talking disconnectedly about a host of things that it would be pointless to repeat here. He recalled his childhood and youth with touching vividness, and seemed to lay no store by what I rashly called his art. The rage he displayed when speaking of what he admittedly loved best of all was sincere, that I could not doubt. 'A quite unacceptable overestimate !' he exclaimed with a look of inconceivable ferocity, and the words seemed to me ambiguous, really obscure. Before I left London I saw him twice more, accompanied by Anna and the three gentlemen, who may have been entrusted with the thankless task of warding off unwanted visitors and keeping up the conversations in which he did not wish to participate; he seemed very lifeless. As for Anna, if she had hoped I would faithfully retail to her the conversation which her deliberate absence had made possible, she was doomed to disappointment. But she forbore to question me : perhaps because she had finally renounced hope of making me reconsider my first verdict, which seemed to her far too close to her own.

III

It remains to be told how Frédéric Molieri, after a mysterious inner odyssey about which we knew nothing, punished those who had loved him for what he was not, flouted the devotion he had aroused, shattered his own fame into fragments and foundered in a tremendous shipwreck, amidst the fury of an audience gathered to acclaim him.

It is by no means paradoxical to consider this slap in the face of his admirers as the ultimate gesture of a dispossessed man.

The last time I saw him on the stage was also the last on which he appeared there as a singer. It would be interesting to know whether the fact that he enjoyed his first triumph and suffered his first defeat in the role of Don Giovanni corresponded perhaps to some deliberate intention of his, some desire for symmetry. I was not one of those knowing spectators who, from the opening scenes, experienced a sort of uneasiness, which they at first ascribed to their being badly seated or to some defect in the theatre's accoustics; possibly Molieri had once again begun to exercise on me a spell which rendered me oblivious to the inadequacies of his voice, of the increasingly flagrant distortions which he inflicted on the score, as he spurred himself on to uncalled-for feats. It is difficult to say precisely at what point the audience became aware that the great singer was not in his best form, that his performance was deplorably inferior to his reputation. How did it happen that during the interval nobody openly admitted disappointment : was it from modesty or circumspection? It seems that Molieri must have intended to instil doubt, little by little, in the hearts of his audience, then to disturb their judgment by a cunning blend of the highest vocal accomplishment and the most unpardonable faults, until the moment when, resolutely switching to an attitude of provocation and pure rage, he struck the blow which was to turn the whole audience against him. Thus, in the first act he confined himself to distorting, more and more crudely, the character he played, turning Don Giovanni into a twin brother of Leporello, a sort of licentious buffoon, a mean and cruel rascal, an unscrupulous scoundrel who could never be touched by a sense of sin. But here too he took care that the gradual metamorphosis of the great libertine into a bad copy of himself was at first perceptible only to connoisseurs, who muttered their protests while the rest of the audience was still applauding on trust; he brought Don Giovanni down, step by step, to the lowest level of abjectness, where crime is stripped of any sort of nobility or courage and can inspire nothing but disgust. But in order to emasculate the

character, to despoil it of its solar grandeur, to give to all Don
Giovanni's actions, even his supreme defiance, a hybrid quality
midway between cowardice and arrogance, Molieri was forced
to attack Mozart's music itself. He set about this systematically, very cautiously to begin with, sometimes by a subtle
failure to synchronise the vocal line with its orchestral commentary, sometimes by over-sweetening his voice, then more
blatantly by introducing and maintaining conventionality
in what had been pure invention, adorning his most famous
arias with flourishes and even indulging in vocal displays that
would hardly have seemed permissible from an interpreter of
Meyerbeer. But proving powerless, in the last scenes of the
graveyard and the Stone Guest, to degrade the music, whose
grandeur withstands corruption, he did not hesitate, in the
last resort, to use the only weapon left him : he sang excruci-
atingly out of tune.

The man who provokes anarchy, however, is well aware
that he must perish thereby. Some people may find it strange
that Molieri so coldbloodedly renounced his fame.

It was only during the second act that protests arose loudly
enough to provoke a counter demonstration among those
spectators who were still favourably disposed, and this happened so inopportunely that the actor, amazed at being
interrupted in the middle of his singing by a burst of applause
which he considered premature, shrugged his shoulders with
a grimace of disgust, which was scarcely calculated to win
him fresh supporters and promptly alienated many of those
who had taken his side. Quite unperturbed by the whistling
and jeers that arose from every corner of the house, he seemed
indeed to be spurred on by these to ever greater excesses, carry-

ing temerity and bad taste to the point of bringing a sob into his voice to underline the pathos of the scene where Don Giovanni defies the Commendatore's statues, or again, during the following scene, indulging in frenzied transports, flinging up his arms to heaven and throwing back his head with the vehemence of a ham actor concerned to impress his audience with cheap effects rather than to interpret his role correctly.

But in the midst of all these anarchical excesses, and although reduced to a mere puppet, Molieri still impressed me by his dreadful and disquieting energy. I admired the sombre ardour with which he deliberately sought to provoke a scandal, to topple from his pinnacle, to degrade a masterpiece to which he owed his first triumph, as well as the courage which, in my opinion, he displayed by facing this horde of aesthetes, furious at having been robbed of the few hours of facile exaltation for which they now felt they had paid too dearly. He succeeded in giving to the spectacle of his downfall—which here assumed the appearance of a freely accepted sacrifice and, as it were, a tremendous settling of accounts—the same character, that of a magical ceremony, carefully prepared, which two years earlier had marked his dazzling rise to fame, and his voice itself, although it had lost its purity, its accuracy, its power, seemed all the more moving on that account, like the voice of an old prima donna in which we can still hear, rising from a remote past, the sounds that had so deeply stirred us when it was not yet cracked by age. Molieri, then, was not the great libertine who, although the touch of the stone hand has brought him the clearest revelation of death and sin, flings nonetheless in the petrified face of the huge avenging statue his glorious, five times reiterated defiance; he was a depraved

man blinded by his lust for pleasure to the point of denying
whatever awakens his awareness of wrongdoing. The cries of
no with which he replied to the Statue's implacable summons
broke off into bursts of laughter; there was no bravery about
this refusal to reform, which he took as a trivial game; the
great figure that moved and spoke with such solemnity was
only a phantom at which he could not help laughing, a trick
played on his senses by excess of food and wine, and thus he
laughed—a laugh of utter incredulity, while with his hand
clasped by the icy hand he pretended to be dying of terror.
'Che smania! Che inferno! Che terror! Ah!' He sang these
last words, and even the ultimate scream, in the mocking tone
of one who does not believe what he is saying and is frighten-
ing himself for fun. It was an appalling sacrilege, a scandalous
outrage which earned him the hisses and hoots of an infuriated
audience, while he gesticulated amidst the flames and, like a
clown in a farce, sank into the abyss of doom, which may itself
have been no more than a drunkard's nightmare.

*'Ah, dov'è il perfido, dov'è l'indegno? Tutto il mio sdegno
sfogar io vo!'* sang the accusing quartet at the opening of the
final scene, which forms a kind of moral commentary on the
drama: there was laughter and applause, while murmurs of
approval greeted the words sung by Elvira and then repeated
by the chorus: *'Ah, certo è l'ombra che l'incontro!'* But had
Molieri, on this occasion, been merely the shadow of himself?
Might it not be said, on the contrary, that he had never revealed so publicly, or pushed to such an extreme, that which
formed the basis of his powerful nature: his rebelliousness and
his hatred of falsehood, which he felt he had hitherto served
too obsequiously? For this deliberate insurrection had first

L

of all been directed against himself, whatever price he might
have to pay, whatever risk he might run from the fact; the
surprising deformation of his voice, the horribly discordant
sounds he had produced were like symptoms of a more deep-
seated evil, which he had determined to expose in the glare of
the footlights, not merely in a spirit of blasphemy but in order
to overthrow the odious edifice of his own renown, in order to
ruin himself irremediably in the opinion of those who praised
him for that which deserved no praise and loved him only
for what he was not .

(I do not deny that my interpretation is a conjectural one,
as indeed were all those others based on the hypothesis of a
prolonged imposture, which the memory of so many amazing
feats renders untenable.* There may indeed be a flagrant contradiction between the spirit of subversiveness which inspired
this calculated sabotage and what we know in other con-
nections of Molieri's modesty, which took the form for so
long of an insurmountable reluctance to appear in public. But
may not the puzzle that his case presents be susceptible of two
or even three interpretations? I do not intend to impose my
own, I do not consider it a final one—there will never be a
final one—but it seems to me less jarring, more in keeping
with the man's character.)

*There were some critics who asserted that they had been taken in,
up to this point, by a very clever actor who, by using with consum-
mate skill certain purely theatrical formulae, had succeeded in concealing
from the audience the inadequacy of his vocal resources: and that the
audience, hypnotised by the expressive power of a whole set of gestures
and attitudes, had found themselves compelled, as it were, to confuse
the singer's voice (a quite unremarkable one in these critics' opinion) and
the actor's performance, wrongly attributing to the former the merits of
the latter. If these gentlemen are to be believed, they were subject to a
sensory illusion: they thought they heard what they only saw.

I stood still for a long time, deep in thought, watching the stream of men in evening dress and glittering ladies spill out over the great staircase as if they were fleeing from some cataclysm, and I may have been hoping to catch sight of someone who would come up to me and ask me to walk home with them: to have beside me some friend or even some casual acquaintance, with his breath steaming in the icy air, and to talk about anything under the sun, provided *that* was only mentioned in the lightest tones, which would reduce it to an insignificant misadventure; or else to go up to Molieri at the stage door and force myself upon him; if I could only see once again the little man's expressionless face and hear his impersonal voice, my curiosity would be satisfied, the business would be settled, my disquiet allayed! But I knew already that I should leave the Opera with no other company than my own; there was nobody left on the steps and the doors were being locked behind me. I hung about the streets for a little while to prolong my chances. That night, in the unbearable lucidity of insomnia, I understood Anna's torments, her intoxication and her disgust.

IV

A few days later I met Molieri in the underground Aquarium. He brushed past me in the dank, greenish halflight, apologised and made no attempt to avoid recognising me; neither defiant nor embarrassed, he seemed indeed quite glad to meet me again. As for me, now that I no longer felt the *need* to see him, how was I to escape from so delicate a situation? He dragged me along to a glass tank in which a debonair

and chubby fish was yawning; he broke into a quite unexpected childish laugh, then passing on to the next fish, which
had a scornful mouth and the bloodshot eyes of a bull, he
laughed again and, pressing his forehead against the glass,
mimicked it like a small boy, smacking his jaws. This disconcerting prank made him seem a different man. Did not his
gaiety imply : forget all you know about me, think of me as
a nondescript fellow without a past, a child whom fishes fasci-
nate and amuse ! But once we had left the Aquarium he lost
all his youthfulness. In broad daylight I thought him seedy-
looking, though his expression was calm and his glance
animated. He suggested lunching together, and the strange
thing was that I accepted his rash challenge, as though to
refuse it would have been far more than lack of courtesy
—would indeed have been rank cowardice. In retrospect I
think we should each have needed greater courage still—or a
greater power of indifference?—to forgo the opportunity that
chance offered us.

'Have you really given up singing?'

The question was a bold one, and I promptly blushed as
though I had uttered some impropriety. I heard him mutter :
'Give up, give up . . . that's a journalist's expression; they turn
everything into their own language ! Give up, what nonsense !'
He turned to me with a smile : 'If you couldn't walk any more,
would you go on walking? It's quite clear : I can't sing any
more, so I've stopped singing. But is that giving it up?'

There was no bitterness in his voice nor any anger, but a
sort of brutal frankness, as if he wanted to exhaust the question in a few words—and perhaps, too, a suspicious haste to
have finished with it. This very frankness ought to have com-

manded my respect, and yet I pushed on more tactlessly than ever (for I too was anxious to have done with it, and this was a task which I performed without enthusiasm, out of loyalty to the memory of my agony of the other night).

'But doesn't it distress you?'

'That's a superfluous question!' he said ironically.

I persisted with the strange audacity that springs from indifference, from unfeelingness (for since I longed passionately for his reply I dreaded his refusing it out of mistrust): 'And why superfluous?'

'Because any answer would be equally superfluous. How can our finest dreams alter the situation if we are powerless to realise them? I may be suffering from this privation, but that doesn't matter in the least, it's of interest to nobody.'

'Except to me perhaps,' I retorted without conviction.

'Nonsense! Not to you either.'

'Nor to Anna Fercovitz?'

He stopped and shrugged his shoulders. 'What an idea! Your friend is happy now, she's free! Her feeling for me was only a whim, she'll tell you so, a whim of which she's surely not very proud. I did her a great service the other evening . . .' he added in a mischievous voice.

'So it was a sacrifice then?' I was impelled by a crazy temerity which did not spring from curiosity alone, and I knew that I was capable of going even further, that nothing would be able to stop me. But for the first time I saw him make a gesture of impatience: 'You're very wide of the mark! I may as well admit to you, I don't care much for your friend and as for seducing her, I never dreamt of it. I'm not much good at taking advantage of situations.'

'Excuse me, but you did so on at least one occasion. And who would hold that against you?'

He looked at me in amazement: 'On one occasion? Are you alluding to what some idiot called the heaven-sent chance of my first appearance?' He began to laugh: 'No, believe me, that wasn't a chance situation, an opportunity that had to be seized by the forelock, no, no!' he repeated laughing. 'I'm quite ready to take what I'm offered and I'll give it back just as willingly! But in that affair, it seems that somebody other than myself prepared the way very cunningly, perhaps even going so far as housebreaking. . . .'

'So it was a premeditated job?' I asked, with beating heart (all my hopes were pinned to his reply).

'So it's been said,' he answered sulkily, as though ready to retract his words. 'More recently it's been convincingly argued that my last interpretation was copied from that of the very Viennese singer who, by his indisposition one evening, gave me my heaven-sent opportunity. These journalists will say anything. . . .'

'While you yourself say nothing,' I commented bitterly.

'As for you, you're pretty good at getting a fellow to talk when he's nothing to say!'

Without letting myself be disconcerted by his irony, I plunged in deeper still, obsessed to the point of dizziness with this inquiry, although I knew it to be futile and unpleasant.

'Are you capable of not singing any longer?'

'I'm not capable of singing any longer,' he corrected good-humouredly.

'But would you sing if you could?'

He looked at me with an uneasy gaze that might have expressed embarrassment or weariness, possibly boredom: 'I don't like your *ifs*; they seem silly and pointless.'

'Won't you give me an answer?' I cried angrily.

'You see. . . . How can I identify myself with someone I've ceased to be, someone I may perhaps become again later, how can I countenance such play-acting?'

He raised his hand to soften the harshness of his words, and fixing a friendly but searching look on me: 'You're very young, I'm afraid you may be rather too impressionable. . . .'

'I am indeed,' I replied curtly.

'I mean that the least thing affects you. . . . You ought to cultivate more indifference.'

'Is that what you do yourself?' I asked, trying irony in my turn.

'Of course! can't you see that's what makes me so disagreeable?'

I thought, how cleverly he evades the issue! and vowed to myself, no, you shan't get away from me like that.

'So you've injured your throat?' I said quickly, with a naïve hope of taking him by surprise.

'So some people say, and they're not the most foolish ones! An affliction of the larynx, that's just it! That's clear, unambiguous and final!'

'But is that it?' I asked fiercely (I felt suddenly on edge, capable of any sort of violence).

'Is that it?' He burst out laughing, flinging back his head. 'He's incorrigible! Listen to me; it may be that or it may not, but in any case neither you nor I nor anyone else can do anything about it. Let's be cheerful and carefree like Papageno.'

'If it's an incurable disease, will you never be able to sing again?'

'How you keep at it!' he cried goodhumouredly. 'Neither you nor I nor anyone else knows anything about it. Now, please, it's my turn to ask, don't you think we should be ashamed of all this chatter?'

'No,' I said in a frenzy of rage, 'no, you're not going to put me off like that! If it's true that our conversation has only been aimless chatter, whose fault is that? I had only one question to ask you, and a very important one, but you've cunningly got me to ask a dozen, all of which you've answered by jokes or paradoxes or . . . yes, by lies!'

'Keep calm!' he said, patting me on the shoulder. 'How you take it all to heart! How I envy you!'

'You envy me? Another pretty lie,' I shouted angrily. 'I know your indifference is only a sham, it's one of those fine dreams of which you were making fun just now! You act it very well, but you're quite unable to enjoy it, you'll always be like a ruined man moaning over your vanished great moments!'

I broke off breathless, with the blood rushing to my head, appalled by the cruelty of my words; they were theatrical, they went beyond what I had intended, they expressed no conviction. And yet Molieri showed no sign of being either offended or distressed by them.

'That may be so,' he said very gently. 'But about that there's nothing to be said either.'

And suddenly quickening his pace he declared in quite a

different voice, with a note of lively greed : 'What I want now is some good juicy meat! Let's go in here, shall we?'

I remember the meal as a very silent one. Molieri partook of every dish with almost animal avidity; between mouthfuls he would pounce greedily on his glass of wine and gulp it down (we drank three bottles between us). In this place his ugliness and vulgarity were blatantly obvious, but not without his knowledge; he was no doubt as capable of deliberately enhancing his own unattractiveness as of assuming coarse manners to shock the genteel folk around him. Here, seen across the table, he seemed stout and red-faced (and I wonder today at this unlikely picture, which lingers nonetheless in my mind). Neither of us was embarrassed by the languid turn the conversation had taken. I remember nothing of his clumsy jokes, his rambling talk, except for the phrase he flung at me in answer to a question of mine about the three gentlemen in London : 'Oh, forget about them! Leeches!' Sated, half tipsy maybe, I was longing to take my leave or him, my ardour had waned. We were rising from the table when he asked me with unexpected concern whether I was unwell : 'D'you find it too hot in here?'

'You're quite mistaken,' I said, 'I feel perfectly well.'

'Perfectly well? Excuse me, but you don't look well. I was struck by that the first time I saw you. And how worried you seemed! Indeed, it was rather funny; your friend and I were running, and you were running in the opposite direction, and all of us so fast!'

'But I didn't see you running,' I managed to say.

'Didn't you?' He laughed. 'And it was you, a friend of Anna Fercovitz's! Listen to me,' he added in a altered tone. 'I like you, you're an honest reliable fellow, and you're wasting all this time with me, who am nothing of the sort! No, don't protest!' And he bade me an abrupt good-bye.

I do not claim that this sketchy narrative elucidates the mystery of Molieri, nor that the solution of the riddle can be read, by the discerning, in these events, of which I was only an episodic witness. It may even be that, within the limits of my experience, I have omitted, through forgetfulness or lack of insight, to mention points that might have helped to solve a problem which seems to have been deliberately complicated by the critics of the time and by Molieri himself, or else I have set them out so badly as to deprive my evidence of its value. My aim was to clear away some of the mystery surrounding this figure; but have I not perhaps obscured it still further? I may be accused of sometimes twisting my story in the direction most favourable to my thesis—that of premeditation, for instance, being inadequately borne out by the scanty and ambiguous remarks wrested from Molieri during our final interview.

But who, nowadays, cares about Molieri? You have lost interest in his fate, you have forgotten his very name, he is still in your midst, on the scene of his former exploits, and you do not recognise him, fascinated as you are by those who have taken his place, but whom you would soon cease to applaud if they, in their turn, were to show failings. Who would be sharp-eyed enough to pick out that little man in black from among his fellows, whose ear is sensitive enough to follow the faint modulations of the oboe? And in any case, does he want to be pointed out, now that he has regained his humble place, from which he can see everything without being seen? We may suppose that, on the strength of his experience, he now takes a connoisseur's delight in the prowess of your latest favourites. Who now is more expert than he at discerning the petty artifices to which they sometimes have recourse to take in their listeners and disguise their weaknesses? Who knows, he may condemn these stratagems, these dishonest practices; or perhaps he delights in them, as clever tricks played on an ignorant and credulous audience. Any undeserved triumph he greets with a shrug of the shoulders, and suppose, on the the other hand, he feels himself bound by a sort of complicity to these proud counterfeiters? Is listening to a faultless voice a painful ordeal for one who now has at his disposal only the thin reedy note of the oboe, lost in the clash and clatter of the orchestra? Who can tell?

'Look, there, in front of us! A widow!' This strange remark was made, according to an anecdote whose authenticity is unimportant, by Molieri one day when, sitting at a café *terrasse* in company of a friend (perhaps that very violinist thanks to whom he had enjoyed his first triumph) he saw Anna Fercovitz appear on the opposite pavement, walking very slowly, lost in a sombre dream, her head bowed as under the weight of some irremediable grief; Anna, like some splendid chrysanthemum, dazzling and funereal, Anna to whom a noble voice had been so dear that she seemed to be clad in mourning for it.

DISORDERED SILENCE

DISORDERED SILENCE

H E H A D been too young to indulge deliberately in this dangerous and exciting practice. When he grew older he renewed it
only as a challenge to nature, and its effects were then pernicious. Circumstances motivated his heroic resolution, pride
strengthened it—that pride like pure alcohol which in some
boys takes the place of energy. His initial project had been to
disarm a too powerful adversary, to escape out of his reach
by means of cunning silence, and he had found himself on an
unguessed-at path, a way of wonders. His misfortune lay in
achieving this exploit once only. Only once, while still a child,
he had seemed to reach the summit of himself, to step right outside himself, and had thus experienced a truly memorable
ecstasy. He thought he had got hold of something like a talis-
man which could make him proof against mockery, deaf to
censure, he discovered that he could easily escape from bondage on condition of refusing to communicate with those of his
own age who, judging docility the wiser or the easier path,
were scared by his wayward conduct, which evoked so many
trite and dreary sermons and were repaid by so many humiliating punishments.

He kept silence for two months; during the third he fled so
as not to yield to the temptation of breaking his vow, which
when he turned fifteen he was to term childish and extravagant out of chagrin at having only been able to keep it by

running away. Later on, it was only his weakness that he
judged severely. Then other circumstances favoured other
attempts, none of which was ever to revive his original ecstasy :
he concluded from this that any premeditation would lead to
failure and that all retrospection was a snare, and yet let himself be caught in it, drifting with sombre delight ever further
astray.

Later still, he recalled so dimly the first impulse of his resolution that he wore himself out seeking for it, as the missing key
which would once again give him access to what he could not
give a name to—rapture? dizziness? He thought he had partially recovered it, but was surprised at first that it consisted
merely of the recollection of a trivial schoolboy quarrel. However, he endeavoured to reconstruct it in all its details until he
had made it as vivid and rich and clear as the most striking
circumstance of a far more recent past—as the present itself.
Once again he became aware of his futility : to know by heart
the genesis of one's first and only experience by no means enabled one to relive it. It would have been better to forget it
entirely, then he might perhaps have earned the right to experience it a second time.

Thus it was that he let himself be gradually led astray by a
monstrously active memory, which he only allowed to exercise
itself on a precise but limited fragment of his past, casting into
oblivion all that had preceded or followed it. Day by day, night
by night he went over the facts and then carefully set them in
chronological order, until, having finished although by no
means perfected this recapitulation, he was reduced to imagining what he could no longer remember. His senses had at-
rophied at the expense of his indefatigable brain : he grew in-

different to savours and scents (they distracted him from his obsession), his eyes fastened eagerly only on certain childish faces where he seemed to catch a glimpse of his own at the same age. He squandered his last energies in this meticulous delirium, to end up like anyone else—feeling stupid and rather weary.

He sees almost physically the scene of his exploit : a series of identical rooms, each of them distinguished only by its dimensions or by the arrangement of the furniture, so uniform that any retrospective inventory is hard to make—staircases, passages, more passages through which, today as of old, he could still find his way without difficulty—a courtyard thronged with children at play, amongst whom he tries to watch the only child whom memory cannot restore to him, since he never saw him, since he never heard his voice as he heard and can still hear, when he chooses, the voices of those others of whom he has forgotten nothing but their names. It is by means of a subterfuge that he gradually evokes a picture of the chief protagonist—the child that he was—which is concrete, if not authentic (only the knees, hands and clothes are that; the rest is imaginary): he gives him features and a particular bearing which perhaps he never had; a sulky face, reflecting his sensitive pride. He imagines him as he should have been, if not as he actually was. He shamelessly dwells in this body which never was his own and which, born of a methodically elaborated dream, plays an intruder's part amidst his intact memories; but more real than what was real, more present than that which only belongs to the past, more alive, in short, than that which was really lived, and he forgets even its bast-

M

ard origin. This was his supreme achievement, as it was also the
first symptom of his delirium. That which was false doubtless
contaminated that which was true, but the whole picture assumed the colours of truth.

Here is the outline of his dream-memory, except for a few
variants which affected neither its character nor its structure.
(Only the order of facts might be called in question any day
by the discovery, ever welcome and ever surprising, of a new
link in the chain, to the advantage of chronology. And as for
the feelings he had experienced, if these seemed to acquire fresh
substance with each daily scrutiny, their nature was unvary-
ing : playful innocence, anger, pride, despair, pride again and,
to end with, that which he never experienced again, that which
closed his destiny.) The first sequence consisted only of one
lightning-swift image : a figure distinguished merely by the
attributes of his condition—a black robe, a biretta, clerical
bands—pounces on the child that he was—and such as perhaps he never was—to accuse him of some misdeed, the blame
for which he promptly shifts on to the real culprit, who is
sentenced and punished before he has time to protest in his
turn.

A disagreeable episode over which he never lingered subsequently either to complete it or to improve it, for his remorse,
if he suffered remorse for playing a tell-tale's part, was less
powerful than the childish delight which he took in replying
by insults to the insults he had deserved, and which he still
took, in these latter days, in enumerating them. Next he sees
himself—the flashback is more fictitious, if no less precise,
than the preceding one, whose authenticity was its only merit
—he sees the scowling brows, the forelock bevelled off by the

school hairdresser, who takes advantage of his customers' youth
to scamp his work, he sees the nape close-shaven according to
regulations, he sees the knees gleaming under the desk and he
sees, too, the childish hand shaking as it scribbles in a cross-
ruled notebook some comment inspired by spite or by the
urgent need to assert himself at last by some positive action—
to reach the enemy directly through the chinks in his armour
before the enemy's lance can reach through the chinks in his
own : the anger of his victims will be a sort of homage to his
power, a ringing recognition of his merits. Unless perhaps from
that moment he had understood what path he must take to
reach a splendid isolation where he need fear nobody's attacks.
Unless perhaps, more simply, he had acted out of pure mis-
chief, out of an immoderate love of play, without reckoning,
or else reckoning very clearly, the risks of a public provocation.
Or perhaps to punish himself for having infringed the univer-
sal code of comradeship he had instinctively sought to cut
himself off from the community, to precipitate his downfall by
some infamous action, to expiate his fault by an even blacker
fault, and by means of the only weapons which he could use
with skill. But these various hypotheses, and many more, must
all be rejected, since none of them can be established with certainty. He condemns exegeses, interpretations, whatever is conjectural and uncertain. Since all is known to him, he is not
allowed to doubt anything nor to suppose anything : his task
is to make the past into a perpetual present, his fate—and his
curse—to relive to the verge of madness what was lived
through once and once only.

And it is in order to limit himself to the facts that he allows
his memory full freedom to roam at will within a circumscribed

zone; and, when memory fails him, he resorts uncompromis-
ingly to invention, basically truer than any retrospective
analysis which distorts images, falsifies their nature and dis-
turbs their chronology. Here, limiting oneself to facts means
reexperiencing memories, and, in the third sequence, these
are purely auditory : the theme of the dispute is respected,
although its terms are lost for ever (but memory suppresses
irrelevant details). The scene of the third sequence is the same
as that of the first under a darker, oppressive sky. Four children are quarrelling with a fifth who is indubitably himself, soon
after he has delivered his slanderous document. 'Don't you see
that the little sneak pretends to despise us because he can't
bear being despised by us? When he'd have been wiser to
make himself scarce, what does he do?' 'Challenges the boy
who got a beating in his place !' 'And who blames *me* for not
being beaten in *his* place !' 'For sneaking on him meanly to
avoid a punishment.' 'One that I never deserved.' 'But he
does deserve the one we're going to inflict on him now.' 'The
punishment of hearing us talk about him till he's disgusted with
himself, with his body and soul, with his voice and gestures,
till he wants to die so as to stop being what we shall have
turned him into.' 'Turn me into something other than myself?'
'Without respite, whispering it in his ear wherever silence is
compulsory, saying it out loud wherever we're allowed to talk.'
'You'll never turn me into what you talk about.' 'Our voices
shall haunt his sleeplessness, they will harry him even in his
dreams.' 'You can tell lies till you're tired, I shall still remain
myself for everyone of you, the self of which he will not speak !'
'But for himself he'll be the self that we shall tell him of.' 'And
what if I refused to speak to you ?' 'He who has spoken only

too much already!' 'And what if I refused to listen to you, if I
no longer saw you? And if I were stronger than you, if I . . .
if I. . . .' He cannot utter, or he has forgotten, the word which
would have left his enemies at a loss for an answer; stammer-
ing amidst their sneers, he has a sudden premonitory vision of
what no word can ever express. He stands silent, breathless. He
stands silent, and while seeming moved by a passing fit of sul-
lenness, perhaps he has already made a secret vow of silence.
Because he is slow at repartee, because he hopes by this ruse to
escape the self-contempt into which his schoolfellows plan, by
their cruel voodoo, to drag him down—but above all this silence is a deliberate ascetic exercise : he has to prove himself
worthy of what he has glimpsed, even if this be hard to conjure
up and perhaps already beyond his reach. Tears run down his
cheeks, not tears of humiliation or fear but tears of joy, of a
proud, excessive, almost limitless joy. . . .

He sees, as though in a dream in which the dreamer does not
believe, the unfriendly figures of his persecutors, the courtyard
where the others are at play, sometimes pausing on one foot to
stare at him and burst out laughing in his face, but, strangely
suspended between what he no longer is and what he has not
yet become, he experiences only innocence, pride and delight.
He is actually outside of himself, and can enjoy the situation as
a spectator, and as if he were master rather than victim of it :
their paltry efforts to draw tears from a stone—but he sheds
real tears. . . . And then the clangour of the bell summons them
into school again, brutally destroying his feeling of omnipo-
tence. While he takes his place in the line, all his ecstasy faded,
he weakens for the first time, close-pressed and harrassed by

those who behind his back carry on their cruel rodents' work in whispers. The careful way he wipes away his tears betrays his weakness; once more he is an outcast, he must disguise his shame, wear a brave face under their taunts and, after such a glimpse of glory, let himself be lacerated and besmirched with a pretence of a smile. . . .

Flung down, dispossessed, degraded—but with this differ- ence in him that because he has caught a distant glimpse of the way out, he will submit unflinchingly to whatever comes, in the fourth sequence, like a martyrdom freely endured and even avidly desired because it is a necessary test in the fulfilment of his vow.

The fourth sequence is a complex one, for it consists of an in- calculable number of sequences whose scene is the refectory, whose theme is his martyrdom. Their evolution is too slow, their succession too monotonous for him to recall them in their entirety and in terms of their actual duration. His memory, unable to recapitulate the accidental variations, makes him consider unique what was repeated endlessly, and as endlessly repeated what could not have been the same twice over. Re- experienced at accelerated speed and as it were simultaneously, all these movements are condensed into a single sequence which unfolds in three distinct movements, each representing a decisive stage and illustrating one of the three dominant themes around which his ordeal revolves : sullen anger, soon yielding to something more powerful which will enable him to pass unscathed amidst outrageous insults, a majestic inflexi- bility baffling to his enemies, who see to their amazement any offers of a truce rejected, and finally that euphoria to which his

heroic exploit is to bring him, coinciding as if by magic with
the complete annihilation of those who sought to abuse him :
his ruthless schoolfellows, his harsh teachers.

He sees a room thronged with children sitting silently at
table; above them, on a platform, the masters' table, better
supplied (the room seems larger, no doubt, because of the dim
light, the symmetry, the bareness of the whitewashed walls,
the monotonous regulations, the long lapse of years). He hears
the sound of the wooden clapper that authorises the boys to
unfold their arms, help themselves to food and talk to one
another. He sees, sitting amidst a dozen other children, a
taciturn young boy who seems numbed by the fear of indulging in unnecessary gestures. His bearing is proud, and the
look in his eyes is stormy, hazed over by a deliberate effort not
to focus on anything or anybody : if he were to meet his neighbours' eyes he would doubtless yield to some irresistible impulse
to answer their calumnies and so break his secret vow.

He is able, at the same time, to be that child subjected to
intrusive stares and to watch him playing his mute role, as if
he were also the boy sitting opposite him. For it is as though
in a dream made concrete, in which he is both the central
figure and the sole lucid witness, that he will see a past experience take place again before him, complete and as it were
concentrated, an experience so minutely reconstructed, lived
through again so many times, with such fervour, that no present power can divert his mind from this demented retrospection, as if this had been the only event in his life, and as though
it were to continue unendingly.

He sees on his right the foolish profile of a boy who either
from opportunism or venality (which reigns here in the form

of 'swopping') has become the accomplice of his neighbours, three of whom are in the enemy camp. He hears this boy's shrill mocking laughter punctuate their orchestrated calumnies. Their eyes meet; then he glances at another boy, whose respectful curiosity and almost friendly smile seem to implore him to give up his monotonous strategy. He sees, as though in the background, the faces of other boys leaning forward to watch with varying degres of interest or compassion the stages of his martyrdom. He sees, and he will never cease to see, looming above the triple row of childish heads, that spellbinding image, the pallid face of a master scrutinising him with bleared grey eyes, with all the harsh authority of adults. From the ignoble gaze of this priest he could free himself only by some supreme insolence : a wink (one night he is to free himself by means of a dream-murder, today he frees himself by an imaginary murder which, defying truth and probability, becomes the bloody climax of his dream-memory).

At first, with the impatience to which his own muteness condemns him, he hears them present their savage indictment : when one of them falls short of breath another promptly takes up the tale, bringing fresh charges against a silent defendant. He does nothing to break the ring, reckoning rather wretchedly that he will be out of their reach by the time their aggressive powers have begun to flag, but then wishing on the contrary for the prolongation of his torture, which is to lead him slowly and painfully towards the liberty he has glimpsed. He hears himself endlessly described as tell-tale, traitor, liar; his long-forgotten misdeeds are recalled, his habits, his tricks of speech, his physical or moral defects (real or imaginary, but always exaggerated to raise a laugh at his expense) are publicly exposed, together with baseless accusations intended to goad him on, to force him from his impregnable fortress of silence; his reputation and his dignity both publicly assailed—but to no avail, since far from being besmirched by his torturers, the victim is purified by them, and becomes to them an object of compassion (and then they will implore him to speak, to deliver them from their feeling of impotence) and eventually of silent admiration (they, in their turn, will stand mute, watching humbly, and always vainly, for a word which will restore them to their basic role of friendly playfellows). In the initial phase, however, more than once he is on the verge of tears and is tempted to capitulate, either because their taunts exasperate his nerves or because by the cruel light they shed on him they drive him to denounce himself, to proclaim on some irresistible impulse : *yes, yes, I am what you have said, I am like that,* and even to go one better by raising his own voice above those venomous voices.

Yes, I am like that! but his outward self, less sensitive, less vulnerable, expresses only : *I don't hear you, who are they talking about?* offers only a craggy surface whose fissures are invisible and against which they resentfully see their most violent assaults break in successive waves. Tears of rage, however, when from the high platform the prying gaze of the priest, as he absentmindedly chews the tough school meat, settles on him with sneering, knowing persistence, holds him subject relentlessly, seems to expose him to an incomprehensible threat that makes his heart beat faster and even his knees, under the table, shake uncontrollably.

Here there is a sort of break in this interminable sequence—an episode out of place, or unplaceable, a fragment gone astray in the midst of that monotonous movement which, with its endless repetition, seems to offer no escape.

The refectory is the place preferred above all others for the daily session of slander; at meals the children can talk freely, whereas elsewhere games, study or prayer are compulsory. Forced to sit beside those who were allotted to him as neighbours on the first day of term, he cannot leave his place save by voluntarily incurring one of the customary punishments. He pretends to snigger during the ritual recitation of the *Benedicite,* he is sharply rebuked and sent to kneel down in the middle of the refectory, the rule being that the delinquent must remain thus till the end of the meal, arms folded, face turned towards the prefects' table. The pleasure he feels at the discomfiture of his enemies is promptly dissipated by disgust at having his body thus exhibited and reduced to this humiliating posture, and then by the shame he feels at being humiliated, although by an act of his own will. This disgust and shame are replaced by another torture, which causes him to fling himself suddenly backward, stifling a cry in his hand (he is reprimanded for this double misdemeanour : not keeping still, and unfolding his arms). He sees, he cannot avoid seeing the possessive gaze of the master who, between two mouthfuls, between two draughts of wine, coldly inspects him across the table, like some object with which he can do what he likes when he likes, or do nothing at all, according to his whim. Motionless, spellbound against his will by that priest, who himself seems under a spell, he bows his head, shaken by a tremor of rage, but lifts it again immediately as though to face an executioner. He witnesses his own torment : he sees himself prostrate on the bare floor of the refectory, immolated there, his body from knees to brow offered up to that gloating gaze which he can escape only by closing his eyes; but then he feels a scorching pollution creep all over his body, and when he opens them again the fire spreads to his face, which he is forbidden by rule to turn away or to hide behind his hands, meekly folded under his arms. Now he kneels stiffly erect, his head pushed slightly forward, staring boldly at that massive face with its champing jaws; now he strains and cowers in a vain attempt to escape from its field of vision, if not to annihilate his own body. But in any case his knees remain riveted to the icy floor while the blood rushes to his face, exposed again to the sinister mildness of that gaze in which he seems to see reflected with painful precision his young humiliated body and, shamefully revealed, the most intimate and secret part of him. From this unparalleled ordeal he acquires the notion of a murder, which he will sometimes realise in his dreams and later, more systematically, will introduce into the final sequence, where nothing authentic survives save the reconstructed images of his old obsession.

Another episode breaks into the series of sequences, each one of which seems like the regular repetition of the preceding ones—but on one occasion he is watching the sun gilding the high lozenged windows, on another, which may perhaps be earlier, he is staring at his plate in disgust; sometimes he yields to the temptation of dramatising things, at other times to that of using irony; either he faces the daily ordeal with terror, or else his very muteness, by imposing on him a difficult and heroic attitude, keys up his energy, strengthens his resolution (each recollection has its specific colour and the number and

diversity of them is inexhaustible, so that but for the lapses in
his memory this mental catalogue would be practically infinite).
All these sequences have the common feature of taking place
in an atmosphere of hypertension and brooding storm, except
the sixth, where, amidst the rumble of waves on the shore and
the confused clamour of sea-birds, he hears his own childish
voice, grown harsh and almost too shrill through long silence—
as if it rang out in a solitary place—answer the questions put to
him without malice by a boy of his own age, walking awk-
wardly by his side, hobbling over the shingle. He hears their
rapid steps; he remembers the other's voice, steady, naïve, with
an adolescent huskiness; he sees the blue, inflexible gaze; he
sees the boy's face eagerly turned towards his own as if
to read there the riddle that torments him. It is four in the
afternoon, and they must have been taken for a walk as
far as the sea shore, where a bitter April wind blows in long
gusts.

'How much longer are you going to. . . . Listen, I wanted
to tell you that you oughtn't to. . . .' 'Go on. Don't be frightened. Oh, do go on!' 'Take care. They're very strong, very
cunning, they won't leave you in peace.' 'But you're wrong.
They're ill at ease, and I see that you are too, or why should
you be talking to me, asking me questions in their name?' 'In
their name? But I'm on your side!' 'On my side against them,
and against me too.' 'Then I should be your enemy. Am I
really?' 'Yes, you and all the rest of them.' 'And yet you're
talking to me!' 'As I would talk to them if they spoke to me.
When have they done so? They don't speak to me, they don't
speak about me, I don't know who they're speaking about.
They listen to themselves talking, but who listens to them?'

'But what d'you mean? They're always talking about you!'
'About me or about themselves? Is it really about me they're
talking?' 'Well, it's really you I'm speaking to and you who
are answering me.' 'It's the *me* that you see, yes, and that's the
one that answers you.' 'And can you tell me how I see you?'
'You look at the person in front of you, you go up quite close
to him. . . .' 'And I see that he expects nothing from me nor
from anybody else!' 'And so that's how you see me, when for
them—even for them!—I've already ceased to be the same
person that they wore themselves out slandering every day!
That's where my strength lies, they've lost faith in their own
words and their own words bore them.' 'So you've won?'
'When I shall no longer be what I was or what I am, or what
they'd like to make of me, when they will no longer be able
to talk about me. . . .'

Here he suspects his mind of indulging in some rhetorical
exercise. Owing to his anxiety to reproduce this dialogue in its
original form he subjected it to innumerable variations which
make its authenticity doubtful (the primitive version, before
any retouching, was perhaps the truer), but even if the words
he hears the two children utter were all apocryphal, far from
betraying the meaning of their conversation on that April
Sunday in their fourteenth year, they are its faithful transla-
tion into a language accessible to a man remembering, for the
things he would say today are the things said by the child that
he was. Only natural sounds, objects and figures can be recalled indefinitely without undergoing alteration, thus con-
stituting, with varying degrees of prominence and intensity,
living landmarks in time—the fringe of yellow snow on the
foaming surf, the unwearying crash of the waves, the gun-

wale of a foundered boat, the chafing of his boot round his
ankle, the cries of the birds flying in from sea, their voices, his
own voice with its childish shrillness in the upper register—
all that, surging up from the farthest depths of his memory,
is concerned with the senses instead of appealing first to the
mind, like speech whose concrete value resides in the quality
and intonation of the voice, and in the feelings expressed
rather than in the mode of expression. If the words are not the
same their content is identical, and the present version, although imperfect and no doubt provisional, is only one of the
most approximate among all possible versions. But there remains one sentence which his memory cannot place exactly,
whether because it burst from his childish throat with the
imperious force of a cry, and in terms which display such
childish exaggeration, or because he connects it by mistake with
an occasion on which it might plausibly have been uttered :
And I shall fly away leaving my enemies far behind! Defiant
words, intended at first to impress his hearer and which later
were to disturb him deeply himself, like certain poems whose
logical and grammatical sense appears only after one has delighted in their charm. They did not spring from mere cowardice, perhaps, since they were to be realised literally in the
seventh and eighth sequences where, by a prodigious upward
movement, he escapes from the forces allied to ensure his ruin
and where, if he still remains aware of deadly words and hostile
faces, he does so like a survivor who, from the pinnacle on to
which he has cunningly climbed out of their reach, can let his
eyes roam over the enemies assembled below, powerless to
dislodge him : he rises above vengeance, above hatred, above
threats, above outrages, and as it were by a liberating and

sovereign flight confounds at the same time his masters and those of his schoolfellows who had dared set themselves up as judges over him.

Another Sunday, this time in May, in the chapel where glorious sunshine is ablaze on the incense-clouded tabernacle. In the midst of the choir, whose baroque architecture gives a theatrical solemnity to the ceremony, he sees, from behind, the officiating priest bowed down before the altar, in all the glory of his sacred vestments. He seems himself amongst the white cluster of choirboys forming a semi-circle round the booming organ on which the chaplain performs with one hand, the other, as though disjointed, waving before his face and inscribing in the air, with mannered precision, curves which are sometimes sharply broken off. What he experiences while standing in the middle of the choirboys is, in the first place, that old, elementary exultance always conveyed by communion in song (and though its character is religious, its power makes itself felt over the least religious natures), but also the instinctive fear of letting himself be dominated by it to that point of uncontrolled intoxication where the mind weakens and gives up fighting against that which might cause its downfall. He deliberately makes a pretence of singing, his voice remains discreetly submerged in the choir, but to avoid the reproach of lacking zeal he mimes vocal efforts by a whole set of expressions and muscular movements, with deep breaths at every pause. In his stiff robe whose folds fall over his boots with their clumsily-knotted laces, he is a hieratic figure separated by a great gulf from the profane world that consists of the anonymous crowd of schoolboys in uniform and masters in cassocks,

all reduced to the subordinate role of supernumeraries, while
a secret affinity unites him to the priest who, to perform his all-
important duty with due pomp, assumes the gold-embroidered
chasuble, just as he himself, to sing, puts on the angel-white
alb. When the voices soar up with sweet or acrid sonorities,
upheld by the thunder of the organ, he mingles his own un-
restrainedly, suddenly understanding that it is by active participation in the ceremony that he can best find access to what
the priest would call God, to what nowadays he can give no
name to, all words being weak and inadequate to define the
unique lightning-flash quality of that revelation (and when he
recalls it he has to skirt round the central fact, and certain
details of his recollection may be the result of subsequent ima-
ginings). At that moment something like a rushing wind arises
and space recedes. He feels within himself a vast emptiness,
which is at the same time a plenitude. Impelled, further, by the
unaccustomed power of the incantation whose meaning is no
longer beyond his grasp, he feels himself whirled around and
as it were flung roughly out of space and time into a world
where everything is clear, where all the painful contradictions
that were rending him seem resolved. The sacred song ac-
companies this phenomenon of transference, and although he
is still only one of its more insignificant interpreters, he imagines proudly that the song comes from himself alone—that
he *is* the song. And in fact each time he thinks his voice has
reached its limits it oversteps them still further, as though carried away by an ever-increasing momentum in a dizzy endless
ascent. Making light of difficulties, constantly intensified, his
voice comes to dominate the voices of the other children which
soon he no longer hears, for his own transpierces him to the

bone. And so gradually by a process which he can scarcely
conceive, for it is obscure and magical, his voice becomes the
organ of his power, the token of his victory. What he had
thought only to obtain by a slow systematic practice of silence,
he has suddenly been granted by the unexpected intermediary
of an ancient hymn whose trite theme is the glory of God and
the feebleness of His creatures. But he is no longer feeble, and
it is his own glory that he proclaims with wild, full-throated
prodigality, as if his childish voice had sonorous properties of
unsuspected extent, as if what it was shouting to the heavens
was a bliss made to last for ever. And while, soaring very high
above the choir, it now rings out through the chapel with
authoritative power, his whole person seems to radiate something solar and is clad, as it were, in a mantle of flame. He sees
himself thus, his face like a sleepwalker's and, although his lips
scan the Latin syllables, with a rigidity that seems to come
from within, like some floodlit statue set high up on a pedestal,
its gaze shining out at an inaccessible height; sometimes he
touches his forehead or his eyes, sometimes he lifts his white
robe to scratch his leg, but all such gestures, being a child's,
in no way detract from the dignity of his bearing but on the
contrary enhance it by their homeliness. Influenced perhaps
by some retrospective megalomania he sees all the children
staring awestruck at the child that was himself, and even the
masters, gripped by his voice as though by that of a demiurge,
twisting round on the prayer-stools so as to miss nothing of this
absorbing and disquieting spectacle; the officiating priest himself, hitherto seen only as a figure clad in the sacred chasuble,
twice interrupts the rite he had so rigorously been observing
to turn round, the better to hear the ringing song that draws

N

him with a force like gravity and makes him stumble over the
steps, but instead of gazing at this astonishing singer—in whom
he could scarcely recognise the schoolboy whose every smile,
in class, is an act of irreverence—he closes his eyes and for as
long as he stands facing the congregation keeps them closed,
with his hands raised to face-level and opened wide, as if he
were about to cover his face with them in order to meditate, as
if he were about to weep into the palms of his hands. And
when, fading at last, the young voices die away on an *amen*
which the chaplain sustains and prolongs with a last gesture of
his uplifted finger, the silence is like that of the heavens above
the region of storms. Then the officiating priest turns round
again, but this time according to the rite, and in his thin
affected voice pronounces an *Ite missa est* which seems to
come from a world without grace, and which brings to a
derisory close that service which, for a brief moment, a child
had endowed with superhuman majesty.

When he reaches this climax of his dream-memory, he is
amazed each time at the flagrant inadequacy of his powers
of recollection; he has remembered only its most spectacular
aspect, but almost nothing of its real content, whose ambiguity
springs perhaps from its taking place on two planes, that of
experiment and that of emotion. Unpremeditated, but prepared for by long and painful self-discipline, this assumption
had the convulsive speed of lightning; it eludes his grasp because it had no precedent and no sequel. How could so commonplace a circumstance (choral singing, which is a matter
of pure routine in a church school) produce so decisive an
effect? How did it happen that a dull hymn which he had
sung over a hundred times without fervour served to provoke

so passionate an affirmation? And how could he have raised
his voice so high in such a place without causing a scandal,
above all how could he have defied and denied authority and
its representatives, in the same outburst of happy rebelliousness, thereby attaining to that complete indifference which is
the supreme form of negation? More amazing still was the
kind of magnetic attraction which throughout his song he was
able to exercise over his hearers and which persisted long after
the song had ceased; for from that day a radical reversal of
the situation took place, which turned his most obstinate ad-
versaries into courtiers anxious to regain his favour, and himself into an impenetrable tyrant, forbidden by his vow to grant
favours to any.

Here follows the eighth sequence, preceding the penultimate
one in which a fictitious past takes the place of the real past,
of which he has forgotten everything except that it was more
plausible, less significant, and probably quite unrelated to the
obsessional theme : this misplaced interpolation is justified by
the fact that it contributes to the harmonious symmetry of the
whole, since rigour and exactitude are only means to fix a remembrance, but cease to be effective where the movement is
the important element to be recovered and to be carried
through to its end, which must be tragic. If he sees today, as
if he had actually been there, what he never saw except in
dream, it is because he is the bewitched and docile prey of a
train of irrecusable images, and also because he considers as
not having occurred the fortuitous accidents which, by thwart-
ing the accomplishment of an extreme action, altered the
meaning of an experience closely bound up with death,

and imparted to the course of his destiny an irreparable
deviation.

The time of the eighth sequence, like that of the sixth and
for identical causes, is hypothetical; its setting is a series of
different places.

It is in the cloakroom where he is changing after games that
he sees himself being approached by one of his persecutors
whose name he has lost. He remembers the grey eyes to which
myopia gives an apprehensive look. He hears the boy say what
he is so often to hear repeated in the same or in other words. He
sees him make the gesture which so many others are to make
after him. He sees himself, kneeling down on one knee to un-
lace his boots in silence, deaf to the words of reconciliation and
ignoring the outstretched hand—unshakeably faithful to his
vow. The other boy expresses his discomfiture by a grimace, his
annoyance by a shrug, his anger by turning his back. Twice
more he is to renew his attempt, which will be repeated by all
the rest in turn without success.

It is in the refectory that his neighbour, inaugurating a more
subtle form of tactics, appeals to his reason : muteness is incompatible with communal life, except as a game, and such a
game is wearisome.

It is in the dormitory, long after curfew, that a night-shirted
messenger creeps up to the bed where a voice—possibly the
same voice—once came to whisper horrors which, in con-
formity with his sentence, were to poison his dreams. He sees
the ruffled head close to his own; without surprise, he hears
him make the most surprising of concessions : not only to
acquit him of all previous accusations, but to accuse himself
in the names of his accomplices. Crouching there, timid and

nervous, the boy implores him to absolve them, utters a few unnecessary flatteries and then breaks off as though defeated by the difficulty of his mission.

It is on the occasion of some festival (a splendid meal is served to the pupils, with unwatered wine on the table) that, taking advantage of the prevailing euphoria, another boy laughingly proclaims the absurdity of the quarrel and invites him to quit his exhausting role, to share in the general merriment : he succeeds in making him feel ashamed of his gravity but not in persuading him to break his vow. The excited faces, that laughing attitude which acts as a provocation reveal to him the falseness of his own position, which he would have neither the will nor the wish to maintain were it not that something stronger than pride or suspicion restrains him from coming to terms with them : he feels himself ridiculous, clumsy, unreal, possibly odious, but he is bound by his vow, and this bondage leads him paradoxically to become, throughout a whole interminable meal, the very thing they had tried, and had too quickly given up trying, to make of him : an outsider, a pariah. How, after that, could he avoid performing some irreparable action which would confirm the rupture, sparing him thus the dishonour of breaking his vow? He dreamed of it the following night, and out of this dream, the remembrance of which the years have not blurred, he makes the climax of a childish drama which he lives through again several times a day, every time as if it were the first, almost every time replacing authentic details by plausible details, or choosing a new version, more full of pathos, which his memory calls in question but which his mind exalts to the level of an unquestionable truth.

The final sequence is thus like a dream which repeats exactly the dream he had on the night of that same festival, but it opens with a commonplace incident which in no way belongs to dream : he is scolded for leaving the courtyard without permission; he may, in order to escape from the indefatigable overtures of his former persecutors, have taken refuge in an empty classroom; he may afterwards have been mortified by a public rebuke, and conceived some project of revenge which called forth, by way of compensation, a dream in which he executed it, with this fictitious climax destined to conceal the defects of an incomplete experience. He was not punished, but logic demands that the fear of punishment should have been the prime motive of his act of justice.

He feels a painful throbbing in his breast as his hand closes on the sealed note in which are inscribed the offence of which he is aware and the sentence at which he can guess. He sees, without turning round, that everyone is looking at him with curiosity, with compassion, with terror, as if everyone can fathom his desperate intention. He still has to cross the space between the master's desk and the door into the corridor, where he will drop shame and find fear. His boots scrape over the diamond-shaped tiles. He recapitulates the plan he has conceived, his hand in his pocket fingering the instrument. He thinks the final stage will be less dreadful since he has foreseen all its details; he tells himself over again that he must perform his deed impersonally and deliberately, as his victim would perform his if he were allowed time. In vain he tries to remember the face he will have to confront : instead of allaying his terrors, forgetfulness intensifies them. He climbs the stairs with deliberate slowness to give himself a chance to recall the

sly twist of those lips, the cruel irony of that look which is liable
to restrain his arm, to smite him with inertia (but to imagine
it too precisely might also perhaps mean renouncing his project). He would like to be what he's going to become
immediately, without having to endure an ordeal whose imminence makes it seem insuperable. He reflects proudly that
his feverish tension is that of a hero about to perform a heroic
deed. Then his pride fades away in perplexity and doubt: the
plan was cunningly contrived, but it seems to him unlikely that
reality will coincide with his anticipation. Perhaps this hesti-
ancy serves here to fulfil that natural law by which any
decision is counterbalanced by a contrary decision, any action
by a reaction: it happens sometimes that a man about to
execute an act which involves his future may tremble and
shrink back in terror, just as it happens that his panic may
paradoxically prove his strength, and instead of restraining him
may impel him to accomplish at fever-heat what he had premeditated in cold blood.

He begins to run along a passage, then along another at
right angles to it, then he climbs, four steps at a time, a wind-
ing staircase which leads him to a third, darker passage where,
through the attic windows, he catches sight of the same deserted
courtyard which he had already perceived at different levels
and from different angles. Standing before the door, even more
than the urgent wish to avenge his threatened honour he feels
the need to settle an affair grown tedious. He hears himself
knock at the door. Not only have the circumstances hitherto
been exactly those he had imagined, his shame, his preliminary
weakening, his race along the three passages, his indecision,
his need to be done with the thing and his double knock at the

door, but the circumstances to follow are no less ineluctable : all that is to happen next seems to have already happened. He recognises the surly voice which, from behind the door, bids him enter, he sees again as he has already seen in imagination his fingers trembling on the door-handle—although his fear has left him. The man is standing behind the desk, his head bent, his cassock half unbuttoned, a clay pipe clenched in his great terrible hand, just as the boy had foreseen. That intermittent asthmatic whistling is the very sound he had heard when picturing the scene. He feels no surprise at the mingled smell of eucalyptus and musty books. He has pictured the hand wearily outstretched to take the note which, according to custom, he delivers, but which this time, this last time, will not be handed back to him in quittance of a punishment which he will not have received. He sees the priest clumsily adjust his glasses, let them drop on to his knees and then replace them on his nose, open the note and having read it, feign distress, whereas he really derives entertainment and possibly secret delight from his infamous duty : and the child confirms with satisfaction that all these unforeseeable circumstances are just as he had foreseen them.

Now there occurs a sort of break in the order of his conjectures, but instead of belying it corroborates them. He had foreseen that he would have to endure the burning weight of that gaze which, a few minutes earlier, he could not recall, or else to cancel his plan and lose forever the advantage of the excitement that inspires him : he stands motionless, dumbfounded, fascinated, as though eternalised by terror, scarcely able to slip his hand into his jacket pocket with a view to the final act.

Here his dream becomes disconnected. He remembers that they stood facing one another for a long moment, like dogs immobilised by a sudden enchantment. He sees the priest, with an authoritative gesture, motion him to the bench. He hears his own insolent refusal. Then he sees the priest's face turn haggard and pale, with a frightened sneering laugh. He may have allowed him time to grasp his futile ruler, but not to hit him with it : two powerful thrusts with the penknife forestall that gesture, the cassock splits, the big black body totters and collapses, the spectacles lie smashed on the floor, the lips, with blood streaming from them, stammer a few unintelligible words, perhaps in Latin, the dimmed eyes stare at him now with surprise and without anger. . . .

Steps in the passage remind him that he may not rest yet, despite twelve consecutive sleepless nights spent planning his crime. He closes the knife and puts it in his pocket, buttons up the cassock with a sense of profaning a corpse, picks up the blood-spattered spectacles and lays them carefully on the desk, piously folds the still-warm fingers over the leather handle of the ruler, then, as if the situation were losing all dramatic truth to assume suddenly a grotesque piquancy in his eyes, he bursts out laughing : dead on the field of honour, his weapon in his hand !

On this dubious sarcasm he awakes, finding himself with relief and with disgust in the oppressive world of yesterday, where everything still hangs in abeyance.

He did not sleep that night and, when the first bell roused him from his insomnia, his decision was taken. That is the initial fact which he deliberately eliminates from the final sequence, but which no mental trickery can ever make him forget. Neither the extravagances of imagination nor a concern for rigorous demonstration can mutilate or disguise the past, which remains unalterable. However, he has no compunction about linking to an episode which was entirely dreamed a real episode that followed it several weeks or even months later. Weeks or months in which he bravely maintained his challenge —in which he merely went on dreaming the details of a visionary act, as today he goes on reliving a past experience. Other facts are omitted, which he pretends to forget—which he cannot forget: he says good-bye to his iron bed, he inscribes a solemn and insolent farewell under the last line of his composition, he gives his neighbours at table a smile which is neither scornful nor compliant, but a smile of good-bye. It seems incredible to him that this tedious, commonplace day, with no sense of foreboding about it, should be the day when he is to carry out his plan. He scribbles a confession note, casts a glance, not without melancholy, round those childish faces which he will never see again, but which today he sees, leaves the classroom to which he will never return but which today he haunts at will. Disregarding chronological truth, he dismisses all these acts which he cannot obliterate, in order to link up ingeniously those which are to ensue with those he had accomplished in a previous dream.

He has, thus, to be a young murderer coolly departing after committing his crime. He sees himself close to the door behind which lies the man he has killed, peering down the dark shabby corridor and then making his way along it with a calm deliberate step. If he occasionally remembers being burdened with a suitcase, he sets aside this importunate detail. Unhurried,

he goes down the spiral staircase which a few minutes earlier
he had climbed with feverish haste. Sometimes he manages to
forget that it was in a dream. He sees the green and red tiles in
the deserted gallery slip past under his feet. Meanwhile on the
left a doorway with a pointed arch opens on to a segment of
sunlight from which there suddenly emerges a black figure
holding a breviary. He raises his cap as he passes the priest,
who responds with a friendly smile. The thought of the cap
causes him some slight surprise, and he realises that this chance
encounter did not thwart his plan. With the same patient and
determined step he walks as though he were invisible down the
forty-six steps of the main staircase, where busy pupils are
hurrying up and down. But he cannot see himself passing
through the school gates without remembering somewhat resentfully that other pupils, that same day, passed through them
with impunity. And he cannot hear his footsteps going down
the street without hearing the sound of countless other footsteps on the pavement beside him. How can he give verisimilitude to a series of contradictory actions in which he, who performed them, scarcely believes? How can he believe blindly
in his destiny as a hunted murderer when the murder was only
committed in a dream? Thus certain tenacious images denounce the illusion; his flight is an invention, but it is true in
substance; he was that proud, lonely and hounded child,
spurred on by the fear not of punishment but of perjury.

Jumping on to a tram, choosing the nearest seat so that his
face should not be seen, getting off the tram at the station,
these facts are recorded in his memory, whether the alleged
motive was a lie or an imposture that served to justify his
divagation. So, too, was taking a ticket for a town whose name

he has forgotten, walking up and down the platform in a state of uncontrollable nervous anxiety, exploring the corridor in search of an empty compartment to avoid the risk or having to endure indiscreet questioning. A young couple in each other's arms, a lady in mourning, a boy scout of his own age deep in an improving magazine, a few noisy idiotic soldiers: all insignificant images which assume perhaps an exaggerated prominence in this recurring survey—while others, for some inexplicable reason, reach him as though filtered down from a great distance—but whose very insignificance proves their authenticity. He recalls a solitary traveller smiling at him (but this traveller was clad in black and had a breviary in his lap, but this traveller held out his hand and wished him pleasant holidays in a high, mocking voice, and it was the very voice of the man he had killed).

He is startled out of sleep by a jolt, by something knocking against him, perhaps by a presentiment: outside the window, lights glide past, grow slower, come to a standstill amidst harsh grating noises. He sees on the platform a lady in furs waving her hand, he hears a voice that seems dimmed by the density of night intoning the name of some place familiar to his child's mind; he cannot remember what the name was, but he remembers jumping out of the train as it started to move and running along the platform of the station, which was the one he was bound for, and flinging himself as though by accident into the arms of the lady in furs, who was his mother, and whose voice he can still hear, that gentle merry voice whispering in his ear those touching, possibly foolish words, those words which he repeats to himself indefinitely as if they could instil into him total oblivion of that which is to come, which is almost identical with that which came before, and almost identical with that which will follow after; those three tender words which close the cycle of his circular delirium : my little darling, my little darling. . . .

And now, how does it happen that this last sequence, which marks the definite end of this decisive experiment, seems by its hasty and confused character to confirm the failure of that experiment? To begin with, it is the dubious fruit of contradictory reminiscences, fraudulent improvisations and disordered dreams : a projected flight is combined in it with a projected murder, but certain circumstantial details deny the reality of this murder and this flight, testify to the legality of all his actions (to insinuate that they may have been clandestine and illicit is purely a speculation of his sick mind) which the final image triumphantly confirms : his mother is expecting him at the station, and he feels no surprise at finding himself expected. Next, the experiment itself, to be conclusive, should not have been concluded by so artificial a climax : neither by a dream-murder nor by an imaginary flight, nor even by a prosaic departure for the holidays; to spare oneself the temptation of perjury might seem a confession of weakness, but to excuse that failure today by pretexting circumstances is an act of dishonesty. If this version differs today from the preceding one by minute variations, it has probably nothing in common with the one that opened the series save its setting and its theme; the primitive version was literal, although sketchy, but this one suffers from unreality, for it is the fallacious product of an alchemic process; a fictitious past has already taken the place of a real past, about which he is no longer certain of any-

thing, not even whether it was real. Finally, here for the first
time his introspection has ceased to be a private exercise : instead of being simply an ephemeral evocation like those that
preceded it, each of which was immediately corrected and dissolved by the next, it represents a unique attempt to fulfil a
new and perhaps impossible requirement. Tormented by the
decline of his memory, haunted by the threat of ineluctable
death, he felt impelled to try and communicate to others his
nostalgia in order to ensure its endurance; for the benefit of
others, he has attempted to describe it here. But certain images
of the past are more impossible to express than the pure
products of imagination and dream, and although his experiment escapes any rational reconstruction, the obsessive need
to transmit it and make it convincing took the place of that
of reliving it in detail. His task absorbed him so entirely that he
forgot what had motivated it : he made it an end, not the
means to an end.

To render an integral account of his experiment, excluding
any parasitical reminiscence, to give fresh reality to the fugitive
images of the past by means of an evocative technique whose
effectiveness is lasting only in the realm of words, to exhaust all
the resources of speech not only in reproducing as concretely
as possible the facts as they occurred, but furthermore in
creating for a possible reader a continued illusion of spontane-
ous improvisation and, as it were, active participation in the
irrational work of memory, these were among the duties required of him for the fulfilment of his ambitious project. He
was able to perform none of them. The complexity of the formal problems paralysed his memory, drove him into the unreality of fiction, into the nebulous substance of dream and,

eventually, into wearisome abstraction. He had tried to give
to this experiment, which at least for a time had exalted him
to a height which he practically never reached again, a certain form capable of exciting himself and of being understood
by others : he had to admit to himself that his task consisted not
in relating it, but in justifying his relation : not in fixing its
perishable substance in words but in inventing reasons why it
should be held worthy of being salvaged from oblivion. As
he might perhaps have ended by wearing out his memories by
dint of constantly reliving them, he eventually buried them
under an inextricable profusion of words; he accumulated
superfluous details about trivial circumstances (but elsewhere
he perpetrated several dishonest excisions), neglected or dis-
figured certain decisive episodes, lapsed many times into in-
coherence or tautology, concealed the inadequacies of his draft
by an excess of rhetorical devices, substituted rash conjectures,
sophisticated glosses or flights of impure lyricism for that which
his failing memory too often withheld from him—from that
which leaves one's pen powerless. In almost every case he was
moved by an aesthetic intention rather than a concern for truth.
By giving free rein to his imagination he sometimes lost sight
of his initial design, and he even came to doubt of the reality
of his exploit, of which this is merely a summary and edulcor-
ated version. How could he admit that something which had
so long fed his delirious memory was nothing more than the
hyperbolic reconstruction of a narrowly limited private adventure? He was swayed between an undoubtedly immoderate
hope and a possibly excessive despair.

His continued incapacity either to dominate his obsession
or to produce the slightest approximation to it in writing made

him fear that death would overtake him before he had finished
his interminable task. But through defiance or because he
could not do otherwise, he spent watchful nights trying to
formulate that which is ineffable, to bring order to that which
is irremediably chaotic. And as though he had had the power
to finish that which has no end, to perfect that which is
essentially imperfect, he drew up a last version which he considered final, although it was no less feeble than the previous
sketches : but weakly, painfully, he abandoned the thought of
destroying this one, and dreamed—tried to dream—that he
would perpetuate his obsession. Preoccupied with ensuring its
posthumous prestige, he experienced the ludicrous torments of
the literary man. I am that literary man. I am that maniac.
But I may once have been that child.